PRAISE FOR
AUMA'S LONG RUN

"As moving as it is accessible and informative, Auma's story is illumined by a surprising vision of hope made all the more powerful by its realism, limited nature, and coinciding elements of loss and sacrifice. *Auma's Long Run* is a superb story which will resonate richly in the minds of young readers."

—Kenny Brechner,
Devaney Doak & Garrett Booksellers, Farmington, ME

"*Auma's Long Run* is the perfect vehicle for apprising readers of the history and present dangers of HIV/AIDS in Kenya, while presenting an engaging story. Whether the reader is looking to read a good story or learn something, *Auma's Long Run* will satisfy."

—Jennifer Wills Geraedts,
Beagle and Wolf Books & Bindery, Park Rapids, MN

"Auma is an inspiration and a fighter! This story is about women and courage and not giving up. I am thankful that a story like this can be shared with such honesty and compassion. *Auma's Long Run* helps us to see today's society in a new light. Open this book and experience Auma's beautiful story."

—Shane Mullen,
Left Bank Books, St. Louis, MO

"I found *Auma's Long Run* to be so thoughtful and easy to read while talking about the hard subject of AIDS and death in a way that was informative without being preachy. I'd definitely recommend this book to anyone looking for a strong female lead character."

—Angela Schwesnedl,
Moon Palace Books, Minneapolis, MN

A Book Expo Middle Grade Buzz Pick

AUMA'S
LONG RUN

EUCABETH ODHIAMBO

CAROLRHODA BOOKS

MINNEAPOLIS

Carolrhoda Books
A division of Lerner Publishing Group, Inc.
241 First Avenue North
Minneapolis, MN 55401 USA

For reading levels and more information, look up this title at www.lernerbooks.com.

Cover and interior images: backgrounds: © iStockphoto.com/Jayesh; © iStockphoto.
com/andipantz; © iStockphoto.com/sailorlun; © David Sacks/Stone/Getty Images
(girl running).

Main body text set in Bembo Std regular 12.5/17.
Typeface provided by Monotype Typography.

Library of Congress Cataloging-in-Publication Data

Names: Odhiambo, Eucabeth A., author.
Title: Auma's long run / by Eucabeth Odhiambo.
Description: Minneapolis : Carolrhoda Books, [2017] | Summary: When AIDS
    devastates thirteen-year-old Auma's village in Kenya during the 1980s, Auma
    must choose between staying to help her family and working toward a track
    scholarship that will take her away from home.
Identifiers: LCCN 2016041225 (print) | LCCN 2016058538 (ebook) | ISBN
    9781512448528 (eb pdf) | ISBN 9781512427844 (th : alk. paper)
Subjects: | CYAC: AIDS (Disease)—Fiction. | Running—Fiction. | Blacks—
    Kenya—Fiction. | Kenya—History—20th century—Fiction.
Classification: LCC PZ7.1.O227 (ebook) | LCC PZ7.1.O227 Au 2017 (print) |
    DDC [Fic]—dc23

LC record available at https://lccn.loc.gov/2016041225

Manufactured in the United States of America
1-41505-23366-4/14/2017

This book is dedicated to my mother,
Elizabeth Adhiambo, from whom I acquired
my love of telling stories, and to my father,
Shaphan Dulo, who mentored me and
encouraged me to write.

CHAPTER 1

My very name confirmed that I was special. *Auma* means "a child who is born facedown," and that's how I entered the world. Mama said the midwife thought I was already dead, though she tried everything she could: sucked the mucus from my nose, held me upside down to start me breathing. At last she laid me down and left me for dead.

Then suddenly, Mama sat up. "Give me my child. Let me hold her," she whispered to the midwife, her voice raspy and weak.

The midwife tried to protest: "You're still tired, you can see her later . . ."

"No, I want to hold my baby. Let me hold her," Mama insisted. Her voice grew stronger.

"Here." The midwife put me into Mama's arms. "Sorry, she's not breathing. There's nothing we can do."

Meanwhile, the midwife passed word to Baba, my father, who was waiting just outside our house. He gravely shook his head and wiped away a trickle of tears.

Mama took my lifeless body, wrapped me in her blanket close to her chest, and with thumb and pointer finger gently pushed my mouth open. She blew air into my mouth, and instantly I gave a loud yell as if I had seen the devil. I was alive!

Mama told me she had no idea why she did what she did. "It just came to me," she said.

Everyone in Koromo believed babies like me, born facedown, never make it to their second day of life. I proved them wrong.

Mama said I had more energy than my two younger brothers put together. At two years old I could be seen chasing the chickens all around our family compound, resting only after I made sure they were out of sight. Running had become second nature to me. No one remembers me learning to walk. Too slow.

I ran.

◆◆◆

By the time I was thirteen, everyone knew me as a runner. At school I was one of the fastest on the track. I was expected to perform well for the school track team. But on tryout day just after I started Class Seven, I walked home from KaPeter Primary School in tears.

When I reached our compound, I found Mama and Dani, my grandmother, sitting under the big *jwelu* tree between the kitchen and the main house. The jwelu's shade reached out like the open wings of a big kite in the afternoon sun, offering some relief from Koromo's scorching November sun.

Baby, my little sister, was playing with her maize doll a stone's throw away. My brothers, Juma and Musa, stood like soldiers, straight and tall, waiting for Mama's instructions for their evening chores. Soon she would probably send them to bring our cattle home from the pasture. Our chickens and goats meandered around, lazy in the thick afternoon heat.

I slumped down next to Mama and rubbed my bare, aching feet. Our whole track team raced barefoot, but on days like today I longed for running shoes. Baba always said our feet would get too soft if we had shoes. I knew the real reason we ran barefoot was that even a used pair of running shoes cost nearly 50 shillings, enough money to feed our whole family for a day. Even with the extra income from Baba's city job, coming up with that kind of money for an extra purchase was unlikely.

And running shoes wouldn't have made today's tryouts any less humiliating.

"What's wrong, my child?" Mama asked in alarm, seeing the tears that coursed down my face.

"I came in tenth at tryouts," I said bitterly. "Mr. Ouma gave me a spanking and said it was to remind me to do my best." Before Mama could reply, I burst out, "I'm tired of running. I want to quit."

"What are you talking about?" said Mama. "Today was only tryout day, and already you want to quit?"

"Yes, that's the problem! It's the first day and I'm out of practice. But Mr. Ouma doesn't even take that into consideration. He could at least give me a second chance instead of giving me a beating." At school we could be beaten for almost anything—being late to classes, getting a bad grade, even forgetting to comb our hair. But it seemed especially unfair to be beaten for something I loved—something at which I usually excelled.

After all, I was the reason Mr. Ouma had held tryouts early. Last year, thanks to me, we'd taken home two district trophies, so Mr. Ouma gave the girls' team a lot of attention. This was unusual, since most schools focused on boys' teams.

This year he wanted to get a head start on training for the new year because, as he said, "We have some very promising students and I want to give them extra time to develop their talents." More than once he'd told me I was just the sort of runner who could make a name for KaPeter Primary.

The other girls teased me about Mr. Ouma's intentions, but outside of school and track, I never saw him. I hadn't visited his house to run errands like some of the Class Eight girls who spread rumors about him. Still, I couldn't believe he'd treated me so cruelly today.

"I'm sick of it! I don't want to be on the track team this year."

I looked away as I wiped my tears. I didn't want Juma and Musa to think I was such a baby, even though they looked at me with sympathy.

"Don't talk like that, child." Mama began her usual lecture. "You have a talent the good Lord gave you. Use your running for a good cause."

She paused, and then added in a low voice, "I know there are plenty of things to run from in Koromo."

Her words made me shiver, despite the sun that blazed overhead. What did she mean? Run from what?

I loved our village, with its sprawling landscapes that were painted dark green during the first rains of the year. I loved the darkness of Koromo's nights. If you tried to count the stars overhead you'd be lulled to sleep by the relaxing breezes and sweet songs of the crickets. I liked everything about our home—the narrow path that led to Haha stream, the wooded area where we collected firewood, even the hot dry days when we had to travel for miles to get water. What was there to run away from? My best friend, Abeth, was here, and so was our family—everyone except Baba, who was working in Nairobi, but he returned to visit us at the end of each month.

And why would I want to run from our family compound? The homestead was just fine the way it was, fenced with trees, shrubs, and *sisal* plants lined unevenly around the entire two acres. Our two-roomed, grass-thatched mud hut stood in the center, and off to the side was Dani's smaller hut. The kitchen and the *boma*—the cowshed—sat behind the house, close enough for us to hear if there was any trouble with the cows. We even had a *choo*—an outhouse—a rare luxury. Most people in the village just used the bushes when they had to go.

Dani's voice intruded on my thoughts. "Child, why do you give less when you know you can give more? You deserved that beating from your coach. I ought to give you another one myself." She hit the dirt with her walking stick to emphasize her point. I knew from experience that this was no idle threat. "Your mother is right. Work hard at whatever you do. How else do you think you will make a good life for yourself? Do you want to be stuck here forever?"

It was a trick question. Dani knew I had dreams of becoming a doctor, and that would mean getting a scholarship to attend high school and eventually university in a city far away from here. But after that, of course I would come back to Koromo. I couldn't imagine spending my life anywhere else.

Dani had a very different future in mind for me. She acknowledged that Koromo was a good place but insisted I should marry someone who worked in the city. Dani talked of marriage all the time.

"*You* don't seem to mind being stuck here, Dani,"

I pointed out, though I knew my grandmother disapproved of my talking back to her.

"Well, I had no choice. Kwaru was such a good man I couldn't resist him," she said, trying to hide a smile.

Kwaru, my grandfather, had died many years ago after he was trampled by one of his bulls. Sometimes I think that Dani never recovered from that loss. Baba, her son, told me that he hadn't seen her laugh much after Kwaru was gone.

"But you won't find such a man here these days," Dani went on, turning stern again. "Don't you see how many young men we have buried in this village?" I couldn't deny that. For the past two years, we'd seen far more deaths than usual in Koromo.

But I didn't want to marry someone from outside the village either.

"I don't want you going the way your cousin Tabitha did," Dani continued.

I stiffened. I would *never* end up like Tabitha. "I'm not getting married," I snapped, anger welling inside me. So many girls got married young and ended up poor and miserable. Some of them were even second wives to older men who were already married. How was I ever going to become a doctor if I agreed to that kind of arrangement? Married women didn't go to secondary school, much less university and medical school.

"Respect your grandmother," Mama whispered as she poked my side.

"Oh my child, don't talk like a foolish girl," Dani continued, as if she hadn't heard Mama's warning. "It's our job to find you a good man. And if school activities no longer interest you, perhaps it's time for us to start looking . . ."

"I never said I was tired of school! I'm going to be a doctor someday." It wasn't as far-fetched a dream as Dani thought. I was one of the best students at KaPeter. The only trouble would be affording tuition for higher education. But several of the provincial secondary schools gave out track scholarships to the best primary school runners, and I would be a top contender.

If I stayed on the track team.

Before Dani could scold me for talking out of turn, a familiar voice called out my mother's name. "Mama Auma! Do you have a minute?"

Speak of the devil. Tabitha, her baby strapped to her back, strode through the compound gate and came toward us as if someone was chasing her.

"Tabitha! What brings you this evening?" Mama asked.

"Mika needs malariaquin for his headache and ointment for his leg wound."

Mama kept a small bag of over-the-counter painkillers and malaria medicines that she shared freely with our friends and relatives. But now she looked at Tabitha sharply. "I told you that husband of yours needs to go to the clinic. There's no way he can keep using over-the-counter medicine like that when he has no idea what's wrong. This is the last time I'll give you anything. A doctor needs to look at his wound."

"Yes, Aunty."

Juma fetched Mama's medicine bag and handed Tabitha a bottle of pills.

"Thank you. I'll be back soon." She turned to leave, holding the medicine tightly in one hand, while the other arm held her baby on her back.

"Poor girl, she looks tired," Dani said, folding her arms across her chest, tightening her lips. "That drunk of a husband is not treating my grandchild right."

We often heard Tabitha's husband passing by our gate as late as midnight, singing a high-pitched version of some church song. Juma and Musa had once caught Mika urinating next to our fence while talking to himself. Now I saw my brothers squeezing their eyes shut in an effort not to laugh. I gave them the *look*, a warning that if they laughed I would tell Mama what they were laughing about and they would get a spanking. We'd been taught to respect adults no matter what.

Mama sighed and gently pushed me to get up. "Auma, go and get the pan so we can wash the fish for dinner. See, you can use your running to help me around here." Her white teeth shone against her mahogany skin as she smiled and pressed a piece of *nguru* into my hand.

"Boys, I need you to arrange the pile of firewood behind the kitchen and bring some in for cooking. Then you can get your nguru."

We would do anything for nguru, the caramel-flavored unrefined sugar made from the juices of crushed sugarcane.

Mama turned and started unpacking the potatoes, fish, and spices that she'd brought home from the market. Since it was hard to see well in the dim kitchen with its one tiny window, Mama would do her cooking preparations outside.

I popped the nguru in my mouth, dusted off my

T-shirt, and wiped the sweat off the back of my neck as I got up.

"Oh! Thank you, my child," Mama said with relief when I brought her the pan. I could tell that she was pleased I was still able to run errands for her. Thankfully, today, all she needed was a pan. My sore legs appreciated that. "What would I do without you?" she added.

Though I rarely told her so, I didn't know what *I* would do without Mama. She always praised me, listened to me, and talked to me about things I ought to know. I needed her advice, even if it was sometimes harsh. Mama was the one who gave me the energy to continue, especially on days like today.

"We're done with our chores," Juma and Musa announced, standing at attention again in front of Mama. At eleven, Juma looked tall for his age, his legs long and slender. At nine, Musa was short and stout. "May we take our bath at the stream today? It's not dark yet. Please, please, Mama?"

"I don't know . . ." Mama considered their request as she gutted the fish, thoroughly washing out all the gunk. "Promise you'll get back here before sunset."

"Yes!" they both shouted and ran past me, whooping with excitement.

This evening was perfect for a swim at Haha stream. The water would be refreshing and inviting, and unlike the dry season, there was just enough rain for the stream to flow. I badly wanted to go with my brothers, but I had chores to finish. Besides, I was so sore from today's run and Mr. Ouma's beating that I doubted I could make the half-mile trip before sunset. Tonight I would bathe in our reed washroom behind the choo.

At least I could look forward to talking to Mama while we prepared dinner. She often told me stories of her own childhood, opening up more than most mothers would with their daughters.

"Auma," Mama said when the boys had left and Dani had gone back to her hut. "You keep talking about becoming a doctor. I don't want to discourage you—I want the same for you. But you need to think about what's possible. It's incredibly expensive, all that schooling. Your father's job won't be enough to cover so much extra tuition. Think of something else you might want to be, just in case becoming a doctor doesn't work out."

I pondered that for a moment. In general, women weren't encouraged to pursue higher careers. It was common enough for women to become secretaries, teachers, or nurses. But doctors knew a lot more than nurses. I wanted to know as much as possible.

"I understand, Mama. But I'm determined to be a doctor, so that's what I'll talk about."

She let out a sound that was somewhere between a laugh and a sigh. "That's my girl. You've never been one to give up easily. Which means I can trust you not to give up on your track team, right?"

It was a trick question. As much as Mr. Ouma's spanking had humiliated me, I knew quitting the team wasn't really an option. My whining certainly wasn't going to take me anywhere. If I wanted to make something of myself, I would need to work hard and beat the odds.

I nodded at Mama. "Of course, Mama."

I knew that tomorrow, rain or shine, I'd be the first to line up for track practice, ready to finish in the top spot.

CHAPTER 2

I could hear the low hum of a male voice as I
approached the house after school. Maybe my uncle,
who lived nearby, had come to visit Dani.

As I stepped into the sitting room, I saw my
father lounging on the old sofa.

"Baba!" I exclaimed, rushing over to him.

"Hey! Come here and greet your father!" he said
with a grin.

"You're home early! What's the occasion?"

Baba usually came home only on Friday evenings,
and only at the end of the month. Why was he home
during the week, and in the middle of November?

"Well, I needed a break," Baba replied lightly.
He stretched his sinewy legs out in front of him,
relaxing his back against the sofa. This had been his
sitting place for as long as I could remember. The

stuffing was falling out, but Mama had hidden it so well with crocheted covers that it looked almost as good as new. The way Baba was leaning back made the sofa look very comfortable, but I felt something about Baba was different. He looked thinner. My eyes searched his face and for the first time ever, I saw sadness there.

"How is school?" Baba asked me. "You're on the track team again?"

I nodded. "We're just doing trials right now, but I think I'll be in good shape by the time the real meets start in May."

"Wonderful! Not too many people could catch up with those long legs of yours, I bet." My heart swelled with pride. "And what about your classes? Are you excelling?"

"Yes, Baba, I'm doing well in all my subjects. I think I'll take first or second position in my class this term." Although I had a reputation as the school's fastest runner, I was even prouder of my reputation for being among the smartest. My studies came fairly easy to me. Plus Baba's incentives—shiny pencils, sweets, bubble gum, ink pens, and other gifts he'd bring back from Nairobi—pushed me to get top marks in every class.

"Good," said Baba. "Work hard, my child. These days men are looking for educated girls."

"Aah, Baba! I told you I'm not going to get married."

"Eee!" He winked. "I need many cows. If I educate you well I can ask for ten healthy cows as your bride price."

I could take this from Baba because I knew he was joking. He loved to tease me. When I was tired, he said I walked like an old woman hunting for firewood. But he also encouraged me to grow, to succeed.

"When I become a doctor, I'll be able to buy you as many cows as you want," I retorted playfully.

"Good idea! Or better yet, buy me a car, and I'll drive around the village like an important man." He turned to Mama. "That would be the life, wouldn't it, Mama Auma?"

I laughed and glanced at my mother, who was smiling. She looked through the open doorway and saw Juma and Musa running toward the house. "Here are the boys, finally catching up to Auma," she announced.

They ran through the door and stopped sharply, right in front of Baba.

"Ha, man, how are you?" Baba said, taking Juma's hand in a hard manly grip.

"Good!" he responded, then moved back to let Musa come forward and shake Baba's hand as well.

"And you, man?" My father's handshake was so strong that Musa almost lost his balance, but Baba kept him from falling. Musa giggled uncontrollably.

"Baba!" Baby squealed, running toward him, dressed in the new school uniform he had bought for her a year earlier. Mama had scolded him for doing so, saying she would outgrow the dress before next January when she started Class One, but Baba laughed and said the sight of his Baby in a big girl's uniform made him proud. I watched Baby throw her arms around him, smiling at the sight.

When other village children went to school, they often attended irregularly or might have to quit partway through the term. Since Baba had gotten his job in Nairobi over two years ago, we'd been able to attend school on a regular basis. Baby would enter Class One on schedule, unlike so many other six-year-olds whose families didn't have the money.

Baba's work also allowed Mama to go to the market with more shillings. Still, Mama was careful in spending her money. Anything extra went toward community projects. Mama had helped several other women in the village start small businesses to raise school fees for their children, and Baba donated to other local projects.

Baba's homecoming always was welcome, even if the timing was odd. Baba made us all feel very special. Even Dani, who was usually so stern, lit up when she saw her son. He always had presents for each of us, and we loved listening to his stories. We knew he worked for a shopkeeper, but most of his stories weren't about his job. The city itself was the main character—a strange, busy, unpredictable world full of all sorts of people. One day Baba might run into someone he'd known back in Koromo, like the Bimas' daughter Amina. Another day he'd meet someone from India or Tanzania. I couldn't wait to hear about his latest adventures.

That evening Baba and Mama sat outside near the kitchen talking about family and friends. For long stretches they just sat without talking—Mama cutting vegetables, Baba just gazing into the sky. They seemed happy.

At dinnertime Mama and I brought *ugali*—maize flour cooked into a firm cake—and *sukuma wiki*—kale—to the table, just as we did most days of the week. When I turned thirteen, Mama had made sure I learned how to cook ugali. She said it was a sign of maturity.

Since we only had four folding chairs in the sitting room, Baby and I sat on the floor with Musa, while Juma sat at the table with the adults. Girls were expected to sit on the floor if there weren't enough chairs for everyone. I was used to it, and I was so glad to have Baba home that I didn't mind giving Juma my seat.

"I don't want vegetables," Baby wailed as soon as she put a mouthful of sukuma wiki into her mouth.

"What do you want, child?" Mama asked.

"Nothing!" she whined, sticking out her bottom lip.

"Child, you'd better be thankful you even have sukuma wiki to whine about," Baba said in a warning tone. Baby straightened up. She knew she needed to start eating if she didn't want a spanking.

"In the city, the *chokoras* dig for food in the trash cans or beg for it. You're very lucky you don't go to sleep hungry like those street boys."

"Yes, Baba," Baby whispered sheepishly.

He patted her head gently. "Eat your food so you can go to bed. Maybe you're just sleepy."

"Do you ever talk to the chokoras, Baba?" Juma wanted to know.

"Oh, no, those kids will steal the feet off your body if you even slow down your pace," Baba said. "In fact, last week I was sitting in a park eating my lunch, which was a bag of chips. Some men from my work were taking their lunch break at Jeevanjee Gardens. It's in the middle of downtown so it gets very crowded. There are all sorts of people there—job seekers resting from pounding the pavement, office workers, and tons of lunchtime preachers, all in that small space, each preacher vying for all these people's attention. I had eaten half my chips, and I put down the bag for just a second. When I turned to pick up my chips—they were gone. I mean gone!"

We all gasped in dismay.

"All I could see was a bunch of chokoras running away. They flew out of the park and into the busy streets. They were so fast I could not even begin to think how they got my chips."

"So what did you do?" Musa asked.

"I just let it go," he said. "Actually, we rarely eat chips for lunch. We usually have a soda or something cheaper, but that day I had treated myself. I do that once every two weeks."

"Will you bring chips for me next time, Baba?"

Sometimes Baby was so easy to please.

When Baba didn't answer, Baby asked him again if he'd bring chips.

"Yes, yes, for my Baby, next time." I detected hesitation in Baba's voice. Maybe chips were too expensive?

I suddenly wondered why Baba hadn't brought us any gifts. Out of respect, I made no complaint. But something wasn't right.

After supper we all got ready for bed. While Baba was away, Mama shared their bed with Baby. The rest of us slept on the floor in the sitting room. We shared a thin mattress that sat on top of a mat of woven reeds. Shortly after Baba started the new job, we'd gotten the mattress, which was much nicer than sleeping on the bare mat. Whenever Baba was home, I slept on the sitting room mattress with Baby, and the boys slept in Dani's two-roomed hut. Her hut was much smaller than ours, but I never heard her complain, even when the boys had to sleep there and she lost her privacy.

But tonight, Baba noticed Juma had grown taller than me. "As young men, they should no longer sleep with other adults," he said in a deep voice. "Time for them to start sleeping in the kitchen."

Boys were expected to sleep away from their parents' house as soon as their parents felt they were ready. I loved my parents, but sometimes our traditions seemed so unfair. The kitchen wasn't exactly the most comfortable place to sleep, with the hard-packed mud floor and the smoky cooking smell. From now on I would have to take extra care to clean the kitchen thoroughly after each night's cooking. It seemed that every time I turned around, more work was waiting for me.

I was both sad and happy that night as Musa and Juma marched outside to the kitchen. I was excited that they were becoming strong young men, like Baba, the father we all adored. But I realized that this was just the first of many changes that would begin to separate me from my brothers.

And something else was different too. Something had changed in Baba. As I lay on the mattress with Baby, I remembered a night when we were little. Juma and I had been sent from the main house to get a dish from the kitchen. As soon as we stepped through the kitchen door to get back to the house, a tall dark figure grunted, then yelled "Boo!" and ran past us like a shadow. We both screamed and jumped back into the kitchen. Baba came running to our rescue.

"That was just a night runner," he had explained as he escorted us back to the house.

"Baba, why do night runners scare people?" I'd asked.

"Because they have evil spirits inside them, Auma. It's not a nice thing to do, and they like to do it in the dark when people are most likely to get spooked." I must have looked terrified, so he softened his explanation. "Night runners are normally harmless. If you call out their name or act as if you know who they are, most will run away in embarrassment."

Juma had looked puzzled. "So why didn't you call out a name, Baba?"

"Because I wasn't sure who it was."

After that, we'd slept with the sheets over our heads for weeks. But deep down, we'd felt safe because Baba was here to protect us.

For some reason, his presence didn't make me feel safe tonight. I couldn't shake the feeling that something dark and unfamiliar had followed him into our home.

CHAPTER 3

I arrived home from school a few days later to find the compound empty. It was unusual for everyone to be gone that late in the afternoon. I rushed from our empty house to the garden behind the kitchen.

"Anybody there? Mama, Dani?" I squeezed my way through the millet plants to get to the other end of the garden. Silence.

Just then I saw Juma racing toward the house. "Mama sent me to get a basket," he said, running past me.

"Hey, wait! What's going on?"

"Oh, you don't know? Mika passed this morning."

"You mean Tabitha's Mika?"

"Yes. Everyone's over there."

I paused to listen for those familiar funeral sounds of screaming. Sure enough, the evening breeze soon brought the eerily piercing sounds loud and clear to my ears. How had I missed that on my way from school? Those heart-wrenching sounds. Was I getting used to them? Had I grown numb with so many deaths in the last two years? Men like Stephan, Obare, Tito. Women like Jennifer, Akelo, Lucy. My friend Abeth's parents. The list of names was already too long, and now Mika had joined them.

Supposedly, malaria and typhoid were to blame for all these deaths. But how could such ordinary illnesses suddenly start killing so many more people than usual? I wondered if the adults and the doctors even knew the real cause of all the sickness. If so, they were not telling.

Pastor Joseph said we must accept God's will and pray for the healing of Koromo's people. We were still new to Pastor Joseph's church and teachings—Mama had joined last year, converting us from our traditional Luo beliefs. Maybe that was why I found it hard to simply accept the will of God, and easier to wonder about the cause of Mika's death.

"I have to hurry. Make sure you come," Juma urged, bringing me back to the present. As he sprinted toward the gate I realized he might make a good runner, too.

I slowly made my way toward Tabitha's compound. The rays of the setting sun felt like tongues of fire upon my back. Its hues of orange brightened the sky on its journey down behind the hills. Was the sun angry that there was another death in Koromo? Even if Mika was not my favorite person, he was my cousin's husband and I hated to see Tabitha alone. Everyone knew that losing a husband meant poverty—or else remarriage to a man who already had two or three wives, whether he could support her or not.

By the time I neared Tabitha's grass-thatched hut, there was a good-sized crowd, mostly women, gathered in the yard to mourn Mika's death. Sitting, standing, scattered all over the compound, whispering in small groups. "Such a shame," I overheard Mama Karen, the village gossip, murmuring to one of our other neighbors. "I hear it's like this all over Kenya, not just here in Koromo. People dropping dead without any explanation. Whites don't die without their families knowing why . . ."

Some women were still crying. I looked away from the adults' dripping noses and streams of tears.

I saw my best friend, Abeth, and her grand-mother among the mourners. Abeth hugged me but said nothing. Being here must be hard for her, when she'd so recently lost both her parents. I'd never heard so many people wailing as when Abeth's father died shortly after her mother passed. It was tradition for women to cry loudly in mourning, sometimes for days. The noise and the sorrow could get over-whelming. I couldn't help wishing that the adults wouldn't cry so much—that they wouldn't insist on acting like young children at a time when *their* chil-dren most needed their reassurance.

Fortunately Abeth's grandmother seemed fairly composed. She'd been caring for Abeth and Abeth's little sister, Supa, since their parents' deaths. She greeted me warmly and offered a sad smile. Death might bring most adults to their knees, but not Abeth's dani.

Stepping past Abeth and her grandmother, I cau-tiously walked into the two-room hut. The sitting room was filled with people from the neighborhood. I had promised myself I was not going to cry—I felt that crying would make Tabitha cry, and she had cried enough. But one look at my cousin brought great compassion for her. She looked so forlorn, folded over with her infant sleeping on her lap. When she glanced up, her bloodshot eyes said it all.

As I bent down to hug her, I was overcome by emotions. My knees gave way, and I suddenly fell to Tabitha's feet, my head on her knees, barely missing the baby on her lap. I didn't mean to start sobbing, but the tears just came. Tabitha gently patted my back, telling me it was okay. And as her baby woke, she soothed us both. I had come to comfort her, but here she was comforting me.

Slowly I got up. As was expected, I shook hands with everyone in the room, murmuring my sympathy. "*Mos, mos, mos, mos . . .*"

Outside the hut, Abeth and I sat together in silence for a while, just as we had after her parents' deaths. Remembering now, I felt as if Abeth had died back then as well. As if whatever killed her parents had taken my best friend's spirit along too. Abeth had returned to school after about a month, but she wasn't the same. Perhaps she would never be the same again.

Soon Mama recruited us to help the women with chores around the compound. Relatives and friends were expected to stay with the family for as many days as possible. It was a time of sacrifice. Even though we were Christians now, my family would still participate in the traditional Luo mourning rituals. We would soon have to prepare our own house for guests who would be coming for the burial on the weekend. Our extended family would arrive in the morning. At least I could look forward to seeing our aunts, especially Aunt Mary, Tabitha's mother, who didn't visit us very often.

At last, after I'd carried and fetched for hours, Mama said, "Auma, get your brothers and sister and go home. The rest of us have to stay with Tabitha all night. Give the young ones supper and make sure you're awake in time to get to school." Her eyes were bloodshot, her voice strained by sorrow. She looked as exhausted as I felt.

But there would be no rest for me. Baby was fussing because she had wanted to stay behind and keep playing with Supa, Abeth's four-year-old sister.

"You never let me play enough. Why didn't you let me spend the night with Supa?" She whined all the way home, and I had to pull her by the hand. When we got to our compound she refused to go into the house.

"Get in here." I scooped her into my arms.

"Mama isn't here," she cried.

"Stop fussing and be quiet." I was now out of breath. I put her down and bent close to her face, speaking very firmly. "Look out the window. It's dark outside and there are hyenas looking for food. You don't want to be dinner for any one of them."

That was the best way to get Baby quiet. She stood in the corner, angry with me, but she was too hungry to stay there long. As soon as the table was set she ran and grabbed a chair.

Being in charge was not always as exciting as I sometimes thought. Musa didn't want to eat what I had prepared for supper.

"You're a big boy. Stop acting like a baby. Eat," I said. "Juma will eat your share if you don't." I scooped some sukuma wiki onto his plate. From the corner of my eye I caught Juma making faces at Musa, and before I could stop him, Musa had thrown him a punch. Juma, not wanting to seem weak, threw one back.

"I will not take this," I screamed. "Stop right now! What's gotten into you two? If you don't settle down this instant I will throw you out of the house!"

After that they ate in silence. Either they were ashamed that I'd had to shout at them, or they were waiting to settle scores later. Most boys were too proud to fight in front of girls.

And this was exactly why I didn't want to get married. Getting married meant being in charge of a houseful of children *all the time.* That would be my only job. I'd read books about women who made scientific discoveries and saved lives. I wanted to be one of those women. *That* was the kind of being in charge that appealed to me. Part of me wondered if I was being vain. But part of me thought that as a girl who was born facedown and lived, I was destined for an unusual fate.

CHAPTER 4

My head felt clearer by the time I got to school the next morning. The tall eucalyptus trees seemed to welcome me. They stood tall, like Luo warriors, against the blue sky of Koromo around the school compound. I felt at peace here, where I could read and talk with my friends and run on the track field. It didn't matter that the school buildings were old and run-down. Some walls had holes in them, windows were missing glass.

KaPeter Primary had more than five hundred students, and most of them were gathered on the school grounds already, laughing and shouting. I passed a cluster of Class Eight girls watching some roughhousing boys.

"Hey, Auma!" said my neighbor Sussie as I walked by the group. "Who do you think is cuter, Tito or—"

"Don't care." I held up a hand to stop her. Boys were such a nuisance. The older girls were always talking excitedly about this boy or that, but I didn't understand what on earth was so interesting about them.

"Oh, come on, Auma. You should at least try *talking* to a boy sometime. You might like it!"

I laughed and kept walking. Over my shoulder, I called, "A boy would just slow me down, Sussie." I knew how it worked. It started when you talked to a boy—and ended with having to leave your home with a baby to look after. No, thank you. I already had a Baby to look after.

What did girls and boys do together anyway, outside of school? With all the chores and homework I had, he'd just go to his home and me to mine after school. Anything beyond that seemed to be asking for trouble.

"Auma!" Abeth dashed up to me, quick as lightning. Abeth wasn't just my best friend, she was my running mate. Running the two miles to and from school helped both of us become better runners. Most afternoons we ran home together after class. We were used to finishing first or second at track meets, although I admit I finished in the top spot more often—especially this past year. Since her parents' deaths, Abeth had lost weight and seemed to have less energy. I'd noticed that she hardly ever brought lunch to school, and even though I shared my food with her, I suspected she was struggling to keep up her stamina. Yet she always tried her best.

"Did you finish the writing assignment?" I asked Abeth. Our language teacher, Mrs. Okumu, had asked us to write an essay about the career we'd like to pursue.

"Yes," she laughed. "I wrote about being a marathon runner, like Tegla, imagining it really could happen."

"I know it can." I smiled to reassure her. Of course it was presumptuous to imagine that some girl from Koromo could ever make a living as a runner—especially one as successful as Tegla, who'd run races all over the world. But I was glad Abeth was letting herself dream again. She'd been so withdrawn since her parents' deaths.

"How about you? Did you write about being the next female Kipchoge?"

Being compared to the most famous Kenyan runner made me laugh. "No, I wrote about being a doctor. You know that's what I've wanted to be ever since . . . well, since all the funerals started a few years ago. It's just not fair that so many people have to die without a reason, without knowing why. *Wazungu* don't die without their families knowing why," I added, repeating what I'd heard Mama Karen say after Mika's death. I couldn't believe I was quoting that busybody. But if she was right—if whites didn't suffer like this—we deserved the same. We deserved answers too.

"I thought you'd given up on that doctor dream."

Abeth's words stung. Since her parents' deaths, she seemed to have grown more cynical. She'd confided that she didn't believe Pastor Joseph's Christian teachings. But it was even worse to realize she didn't believe in *me*.

"Besides," Abeth said, resting her hand on my shoulder, "to become a doctor, you'd have to leave Koromo. And we all know Auma is never leaving Koromo!"

Although I laughed, I felt a tugging in my stomach. One side of my belly seemed to twist toward home, while the other half wrenched at everything I wanted to know.

Since it was a cloudy day and the school had no electricity, it was dim inside our classroom—so dim that I had trouble seeing what Mrs. Okumu had written on the crusty old blackboard. "Good morning, Class Seven," Mrs. Okumu greeted us.

"Good morning, Mrs. Okumu," all forty-five students in the class responded in unison.

There were only fifteen girls in my class. The boys had tried to take control, but Mrs. Okumu ran a strict classroom and put them in their place. Whenever they'd start talking out of turn or making smart remarks, the teacher would stop and look straight at the offender. She then would say something like, "Please do not reveal your ignorance in public."

Mrs. Okumu was my favorite teacher because of how well she handled those boys—and because she let me borrow storybooks to take home on weekends. I loved language class almost as much as science class.

"Please take out your essays. We are going to read them out loud, one at a time."

I quickly pulled the sheet of paper from my almost-filled composition book. A boy named Peter was called upon to read his essay first. He pulled out a crinkled piece of ruled paper and stood at his bench. Before he began reading, I saw him shoot a "Here I go" grin toward his friend Tito.

"What I want to be when I grow up," Peter began, reading the title of his essay in a devilishly pleasant voice. "Options in Kenya are limited. My neighbors farm their land from the time the sun comes up until it goes down, and yet they have little to show for it. This will not be me. I've decided I will be a bum instead. A career bum, that is. At no cost to me, I will return home at the end of the day with coins in my cup from tourists who are sure to feel . . ."

Mrs. Okumu snatched his essay and sent him to the headmaster's office. Most of the class was roaring with laughter by now. Only a handful of us kept quiet. One of the girls had a disabled grandfather who begged for money with a cup. I also noticed that Abuya, the boy who sat closest to me, wasn't laughing.

"Settle down, class." Mrs. Okumu rapped the board with her pointer stick, a twisted and thinned piece of wood cut from the *powo* tree behind the schoolyard. Mrs. Okumu called on boy after boy, then girl after girl, to read their essays.

Peter might be a clown, but he was right when

he said that opportunities were limited. All the essays focused on the same handful of realistic career options. Farmer. Market seller. Butcher. One boy wanted to be a priest, and he was ridiculed. Abeth and I would be the last to read. I knew we'd probably be ridiculed, too, because our responses were so different from the rest. I just hoped that my classmates were hot and tired enough that they wouldn't pay attention to yet another boring essay. I only cared that Mrs. Okumu heard my dream.

Mrs. Okumu called on me, and I stood up. I had been confident before, but now I was starting to sweat. My palms were already wet, and I tried to steady my hands so I could read smoothly. I cleared my throat. "When I grow up, which will be very soon—or so I'm told by my grandmother, who plans to marry me off early—I want to become a doctor."

I paused. Silence. No laughter or snickers, so I continued.

"Every day in Koromo it seems we hear the drums. Every day in Koromo, mothers, fathers, even babies die and the doctors can't explain it. Some are quick to say it's malaria, but malaria has plagued us for years. We've never attended so many funerals in one season before. I want to become a doctor. I want to find out what is killing our people, and once I find out, I will work to end it. I believe that if I study hard now, one day the opportunity will come for me to earn my certificate and serve the people of Koromo by racing from home to home, beating death to the finish line."

After I read that last line I let all my breath out. Mrs. Okumu nodded approvingly as I sat back down.

"Good, Auma!" she said. "I can see that you are going to help our community. We need young people who plan on returning."

The class was silent. At first I thought everyone was sleeping or numb from boredom. But Abuya gave me a look that showed kindness in his eyes. My face flushed with pride. If Abuya didn't laugh, maybe it was possible . . .

Now Abeth stood up straight, looking confident that she would get a similar reaction. But as she began to read, Peter came back to the classroom. It wasn't long before he was making faces and mouthing words to the other boys in the corner.

Abeth read, "It is true that there are very few women in Kenya who are runners, but what does it matter? I can be one more woman to make it. My father . . ." She paused, then went on slowly,

"My father used to say, 'Use whatever the good Lord has given you to make a good life for yourself and others.'"

I hoped Abeth would just keep reading and not look up, but when one boy, Francis, couldn't contain a snort, she looked up and saw him make a funny face. I could see her lips trembling. At first I thought she was angry. Maybe she was. But when I saw the tears well up, I knew it was all coming back to her— her parents dying right in front of her, all over again. I closed my eyes, afraid to look at my friend's face.

I took a deep breath. When I opened my eyes, no one was standing in Abeth's spot. She had run out of the classroom.

I wondered for a split second if my mother would consider this a good reason to run, but I decided Abeth was more important than any beating I'd get for ditching class. Mrs. Okumu would understand, wouldn't she?

I sprang to my feet and dashed out, racing after Abeth.

I caught up to her outside the schoolyard, and we walked in silence for a while. We had been friends since Class One. We often gathered firewood together and met up at Haha to wash our laundry, and we always went home from school together—although never before school was over, and something told me we might not be headed for home.

Usually we chatted constantly. But over the last year, things had changed for Abeth, and our trips home had grown quieter.

Abeth broke the silence.

"I can't come to school tomorrow," she said, swallowing hard. "Supa has malaria, and my grandmother wants me to take her to the hospital in Homa Bay. Can you bring me notes and homework assignments tomorrow after school?"

"Of course." I had done this for Abeth before, when she spent weeks out of school after her parents' funerals. I knew how difficult everything had been for Abeth been since her parents died. Because she had to help her grandmother cook, fetch water, or do odd jobs to earn money for food, keeping up at school had become a major challenge. She did her homework by a tiny oil lamp long after the sun had gone down and her many chores were finished.

At times like this, I realized how fortunate I was. Several of our fellow students were also *kiye*—orphans. I never used that word around Abeth or any of the others who'd lost parents. The word was heavy, weighed down by the sadness it carried.

I still couldn't figure out why only parents seemed to be dying, leaving behind healthy grandparents. Some infants had died too, but all of us in between— the Aumas, Abeths, Peters, and Abuyas—remained healthy. Only we seemed to be the ones destined to see the next decade. Unless something changed.

As we walked, I tried my best to encourage Abeth.

"Just think, Abeth: in January you and I will be in Class Eight, the top class in school. Then in another year, we can get scholarships and go to high school."

"Mmm," she hummed in agreement, looking away so I would not see she was crying. As we were about to cross the street toward a clearing, we heard wailing close behind us. The sound made my heart race. We looked at each other and knew what the wailing meant. Someone else had just died.

As if in a trance, everyone on the dirt road slowed down or stopped moving, their eyes searching to see where the sound came from. We both turned to see Mama Awino, my neighbor, running toward us as fast as her legs could carry her. She passed by without turning her head, as if she had no idea who we were.

Her face was twisted, and her eyes didn't blink. Her body leaned forward. She looked like she was going to trip and fall.

Abeth and I said nothing more to each other for the rest of the afternoon. Sometimes friends just needed to be together. Our silence was all the conversation we needed. We lay under a *keyo* tree and stared up into the white clouds softly drifting across the blue sky. The only sound came from the rustling leaves blown by the gentle, soft breeze, which blew steadily from the lake miles away. The tree's shade was thick and cool, a contrast from the hot sun. I don't know how long we had been lying there, but I woke up to Abeth telling me she had to go home.

"Oh, my!" I yelled. I remembered I had to get firewood. I hoped Musa and Juma were still waiting back at school and raced there.

Yes, Baba, I thought to myself as I dodged a mule cart and a woman carrying a tray of stacked bananas atop her head. *My long legs definitely come in handy.*

As I ran, I recalled an assignment Mrs. Okumu had given us soon after Abeth returned to school. We were supposed to write a letter to a friend. Abeth wrote her letter to me.

I'm very grateful. You are my friend forever.

When I read those words, I cried so hard that I smeared the ink. Her letter reassured me that she would be all right.

Bringing my thoughts back to the present, I rounded the corner and was heading toward KaPeter Primary School when another sharp cry sliced my eardrums. Twice in a single day.

Out of respect, I paused. I covered my ears, hoping the cry would stop. I wondered again what was killing these people. Were the deaths connected, or was it all just coincidence?

I could see Juma and Musa resting on the hedge outside the school. I let out a sigh of relief, uncovered my ears, and let my stomach relax.

"Boys, we need to stop for firewood on the way home."

"Can't you go with the other girls?" Juma asked. Normally, my younger brother wouldn't question my orders—just as I wouldn't question orders from our parents or Dani. But maybe because Baba was home now, and we didn't know for how long, Juma was anxious to race home and spend time with him.

"It's not Sunday. The girls have chores to do. Just come with me. No excuses."

We all headed toward the turn in the road that would lead through the woods. The boys knew Mama didn't want me gathering firewood alone. "You never know who's roaming those woods," she always warned. But I knew who was trouble. Boys, always boys. Why wasn't anyone ever afraid of a girl? Well, they would be if they met *me* in the woods.

♦♦♦

The *snap, snap, snap* of breaking wood echoed through the air as I added the last branches to my pile. It hadn't taken me long to gather enough. I'd been collecting firewood here since I was eight years old, so by now I knew the best places to find dry wood. "Juma, Musa, I'm ready to go. Come help me now," I called. No response. I listened for a moment and called out again.

Again, silence.

I stepped cautiously and quietly back to the spot where I'd left my brothers playing. As I got closer, I heard voices. I slowed down, tiptoeing from one tree to another as I got closer to the voices. Through the branches I saw a boy talking to my brothers. He looked older than Juma. I squinted, trying to look closer.

I saw Juma making wide gestures with his arms and heard him say, "No, we can't do that!" He looked at Musa, who was hiding behind him.

"Just let me talk to her," the young man insisted, casually tossing a large stick of wood back and forth between his hands.

"What do you want from her?" Juma demanded and clenched his fists at his side.

"Just wait here while I go and talk to her," the boy answered. He started toward the spot where I was hiding.

Juma moved to block his path. "You are not talking to our sister without us."

"Get out of here," the young man said.

Then he hit Juma in the face.

I gasped, but no one turned toward me. Juma quickly recovered his balance and threw a punch at the boy. Musa, who had been quiet the whole time, started kicking the boy and swinging his fists. The boy pushed Musa away, then locked Juma into a wrestle. "You stay away from my sister!" Juma shouted as they both tumbled into a leafy shrub.

Hearing those words, I felt energy surge through my veins. My brothers were willing to fight for me. I couldn't let them fight alone.

I lurched from the bushes as Juma and the boy stumbled back to their feet.

"Hey!" I ran right up to the boy and yelled in his face, "Stop hitting my brothers! I'll call our father!"

Right then, I realized that his face was familiar, but I couldn't recall where I'd seen him.

At the mention of my father, his eyes widened. He backed away.

"Let us never see you here again, understand?" I shouted after him, wishing my voice was deeper. He turned and walked off, not looking back. I took a deep breath, trying to settle my rage and fear.

"I think he wanted to hurt you," Juma said. "Come on, let's get the firewood and get out of here before he comes back."

"Do you know him, Auma?" asked Musa as we made our way down the path through the undergrowth.

I shook my head. "But I know his face," I muttered, mostly to myself. "Well, maybe it will come back to me."

By the time we got home, I had remembered who the boy was. I couldn't recall his name, but we had been together in Class Three. He had left my school a couple of years ago, after his parents died, and I hadn't seen him since. Mama and I had attended their funeral. Rumor had it that his parents were poisoned. "That's not true," Mama had whispered to me during the funeral.

Now, I rushed over to Mama and told her what had happened in the woods.

She looked grim. "This just goes to show why you should never fetch firewood without either your brothers or a group of other girls. I know you're tough, Auma, but extra security is always good."

I nodded. But now I had something else weighing on my mind. "Mama, you told me that boy's parents weren't poisoned, but you never told me what really killed them."

"Ah, I don't know." She waved her hand, dismissing my question. "I just didn't believe the rumors of poisoning. But life is very unpredictable, and who knows what people do out there."

"But Mama, people are really dying. Is it normal? Until the last year or two, I recall only one uncle dying when I was five or six, and then a neighbor about a year later. Lately, we often bury three people in one day, in this village alone."

"Child, that's a hard question to answer," she said, throwing small sticks into the fire.

"But don't the doctors normally know what kills a person?"

"Auma." Mama looked directly at me, which meant I needed to shut up. "I would tell you if I knew anything for sure."

It was hard to argue with that. But Mama had never treated me this way before—deflecting my questions instead of answering them fully. I sensed that she wasn't telling me everything she knew. Did she think I was too young to understand?

"Now get me a cooking pot. We don't want to eat too late," Mama said, quickly changing the subject. "Your father is home and I'm sure we'll all want plenty of time to spend with him."

I was not going to get more out of Mama.

CHAPTER 5

Two days later, on Wednesday, I woke up just before the golden sun spilled over the low rolling hills, ready to make a trip to Haha stream.

"Easy, child," said Mama as I leaped up from my mat. "A woman should awaken gently."

As if anyone can control how they wake up!

"When your future husband sees you leap up like that, he'll think you're possessed by evil spirits!"

I just laughed at that. A few minutes later I was on my way to the stream with our plastic water bucket.

Because I was the eldest female, fetching water was my responsibility. I didn't mind. Carrying a large bucket full of water was a small price to pay for watching the sunshine reflecting off the stream, or witnessing a deer as she lowered her head to drink from Haha.

I especially loved this time of year, just after the rains were over. I enjoyed the trickling sounds of the water spilling over the bedrock, knowing that in a few weeks, the stream would be parched, and we would have to dig *sokos* in the sand again to get our water.

On the path back to my house, I noticed how tall and slim my shadow looked, especially with the addition of a bucket on top of my head. But Dani said I was "filling out." Most girls in my class couldn't wait to become women, but I preferred things as they were. I didn't even want to grow my hair out, like some of the girls talked about doing. Short hair was easier to care for, and it seemed to draw less attention from boys. I thought of what Mama had said this morning. I wouldn't mind men thinking I was possessed by evil spirits, if it meant I could be myself.

When school let out that afternoon, I grabbed my book bag and ran most of the way home. Every Wednesday Mama sent me to the weekly market at the local shopping center, another chore that I loved.

As usual, Mama was using Juma's pencil to make the shopping list, writing slowly in the neatest penmanship I'd ever seen. It took Mama quite some time to write the list—not because it was long, but because she'd dropped out of school in Class Four and writing didn't come easily to her. Once, when I was in a rush to get to the market, I'd told her to just let me write it, that I would be so much faster. Mama didn't cry, but she'd looked as though I had knocked the wind out of her. I hadn't meant to insult her, but the guilt still panged me when I thought of that day. As Mama made her weekly list, I complimented her penmanship and practiced my patience, which Pastor Joseph said is a virtue.

The items were listed in the order she wanted me to buy them. I was to start with the shop at the outskirts of the market, and then move on to the open-air stalls. Mama would always remind me to check with her friends first before buying from others. Last time I was at the market, I'd realized two of Mama's favorite vendors were no longer there. The ladies had passed, leaving their usual spots empty.

Mama's list always consisted of cooking oil, matches, fish, vegetables, bananas, sweet potatoes, and paraffin. I could see her finishing her perfect *n* on *paraffin*, and then she handed me the paper. I reached to take it from her, but Mama didn't let go.

Always she gave me the same instructions. "Make sure you don't stop and talk to anyone, especially those market boys. Be back in an hour, or else I'll think that you're playing." Then she reminded me to guard the money from pickpockets. Finally she said, "Take the basket and run."

No one had to tell me twice to run.

Sometimes I thought Mama treated me like I was much younger and less responsible than I really was. I especially felt that way when she avoided answering my questions. Still, I was looking forward to my trip to the market.

The road to the shopping center was teeming with people—mostly women carrying empty baskets. Buying produce was a woman's job. Like the other women, I balanced my basket on my head to avoid the risk of having it knocked out of my hands by the jostling crowd.

Near the shopping center, a handful of young men idled outside the market enclosure, like hawks circling to snatch a chick. Some would be talking to their girlfriends, while others tried to get the attention of passing girls. Mama had always made it clear to me that boys were off-limits, so I ignored them as I passed through into the open-air market.

Inside, people clogged the narrow paths, careful not to step on produce arranged on the ground. A dusty haze settled over everything as vans made their stops to let traders off-load their goods. Stall vendors—also mostly women—tried to draw attention to their goods. Some men visited the cattle side of the market. A small crowd of men stood around a big shade tree watching an *ajwa* game, craning to see the board.

As I picked my way through the crowd, I spied Mama Karen and her friend Nyar Kano walking just ahead of me. These were the kind of women who "sniffed for gossip like dogs around roasting meat," as Abeth would say. Mama and Pastor Joseph always said gossiping wasn't right, but during my trips to the market I often found that *listening* to gossip was a difficult temptation to resist.

I followed the two ladies at a safe distance, close enough to hear what they were saying, yet far enough so no one would suspect me of eavesdropping.

"Have you heard the latest?" Mama Karen asked her friend. "The nurses at the Homa Bay hospital are saying that all these people who've died in the village died from this new disease called AIDS."

I had never heard of this disease before.

"Some people are calling it Slim," added Mama Karen.

This was a name I recognized, though I'd only heard it spoken a handful of times. Pastor Joseph had mentioned it a few weeks ago at church, when he talked of the importance of a virtuous life. Slim was a dirty disease, he said, and only sinners got it. Those who died from Slim were being punished for disobeying God's commands. It hadn't occurred to me that he could be talking about the same illness that was striking down so many of our neighbors.

"No, really?" Nyar Kano covered her mouth and stopped walking abruptly. I had to stop, too, or I would have clipped her heels. "Where did you hear that?"

"I go to the hospital regularly." Mama Karen seemed to go everywhere, and quite often. It was annoying sometimes how much of everyone's business she knew. I hoped my family had remained out of her gossip.

"Do the doctors have a cure?"

"No, though I hear that the medicine man claims

to have treated some people successfully."

I bit back a gasp. The medicine man lived on the outskirts of the village. I'd heard that he claimed to cure all sorts of diseases—but with strange methods, using everything from herbs to live animals. And sometimes people had to do strange things in the name of healing. Pastor Joseph said the medicine man's ways were unholy and dangerous.

Mama Karen went on, "Apparently a doctor scholar from England has written that when you have this disease, you don't actually die from it, but it makes your body so weak that even a cold can kill you. So it's very mysterious, and the dead are often misdiagnosed."

I didn't know anything about Slim, but I was almost positive Mama Karen was just making up one of her stories again. To claim that most people in the village had died because of this sinner's disease—that was insane. The people of Koromo weren't dirty people. Those who had died had lived decent lives. Like Abeth's parents. Like our neighbor Mama Awino's husband. Like the infant who was buried last week.

Well, Tabitha's husband was a drunkard, so maybe that was his sin if Slim had caused his death . . .

"Listen, my dear," continued Mama Karen, "the nurse at St. Joseph's said that it's very common for people to die of . . . you know . . . without ever knowing they had it."

"You mean I could have it and not be aware?" Nyar Kano's eyes grew wider.

"Yes, yes, sometimes," Mama Karen nodded.

"How do people get it?"

"Are you that ignorant? You'll get it if you 'walk around.' And you can imagine how many of our men who work in the cities forget their vows to their wives and start keeping company with other ladies. Or how many wives get bored while their husbands are away from home . . . All the ways to get it are quite dirty, in fact, but I'm sure *you* have nothing to worry about."

Mama Karen said this more like a question than a statement of reassurance. She was probably fishing for more gossip, to see if Nyar Kano had ever done anything sinful. Whether Nyar Kano had or not, I knew she wouldn't discuss such a private matter openly. No one ever talked about such things, especially in public.

"But plenty of people who have died never 'walked around,' surely," Nyar Kano said. "You know ladies like Jecinta were as virtuous as the Lord makes women."

"My dear, that's where I'm also confused. But in my many years of life I've discovered many virtuous people who have secrets, devilish secrets. Who knows what our neighbors are really up to when we can't see them?"

My mind started racing. At home, no one had told me anything about sex. But I was old enough to recognize the veiled ways adults talked about it among themselves, even if I still didn't really know what they meant. Mama called it "sinning with a man." Others called it "walking around." If there was any truth to what Mama Karen was saying, that would mean that Abeth's parents . . .

No, it couldn't be true. Did Mama and Baba know anything about Slim? About . . . AIDS?

I was so lost in thought that I didn't notice when I stepped right on Mama Karen's heels.

"Auma!" Mama Karen dragged out my name in a way I didn't like and then turned to Nyar Kano and said, "This is Simu Onyango's eldest daughter."

"Eee . . . Simu's firstborn?"

"Yes ma'am," I said respectfully, casting my eyes down at a ripped plastic bag under my feet—one of many that littered the cluttered path. The three of us kept walking side by side.

"How is your mother?"

"She's well, thank you."

I kept my responses as short as possible. I didn't want to reveal anything to Mama Karen that she could turn into a story, like the fact that I'd skipped school yesterday. Baba and Mama always joked that whatever Mama Karen knew by breakfast, all of Koromo would know by supper.

"Did I see your father come home last week?"

"Yes, ma'am." I started to walk a little faster, dodging the broken Coca-Cola bottles and piles of trash. I sensed that more questions were coming, and I didn't want to talk anymore. As politely as I could manage, I said, "Excuse me, I have to walk fast. I'll miss the fish if I don't hurry."

I increased my speed, rushing past them.

I collected my market goods in record time and ran all the way back home.

"How was the market?" Mama asked.

"Fine," I said, and went to retrieve my school uniform from the clothesline before the cows came home. One of our cows had a bad habit of eating cloth.

I wanted to ask Mama about AIDS but didn't know where to start. Asking Baba might get me somewhere, though. He'd spent a lot of time in the city, so he might have heard more about this disease than Mama had.

Besides, I missed talking to Baba. Usually when he was home, we took long walks together to visit relatives' homes as far as two hours away. We would chat all the way to our destination. I especially enjoyed his stories about Nairobi. He made the city seem so complex—a place where one would get lost, but also a place that was full of possibilities. Somehow the more I listened the more I felt like I was looking into another world from my window, slowly recognizing places and meeting people.

He'd be able to tell me about AIDS if anyone could.

"Mama, where's Baba?" I asked when I came back inside.

"Sleeping," she replied quickly, "and don't wake him up."

It was terribly odd for my father to be sleeping that early in the evening, especially on a Wednesday afternoon. Maybe he would answer my questions once he woke up.

But Baba slept through dinner. That night I went to bed without speaking to him, and my questions remained unanswered.

◆◆◆

"Is Abeth out again?" asked Abuya as we all took our seats for language class the next morning.

"Hm?" My mind had been wandering. "Oh— yes, looks like it." Abeth had been gone for several days now. Poor Supa must still have malaria. Their grandmother would need Abeth's help to take care of a sick child and keep up with household chores at the same time.

"I hope her sister gets better soon," said Abuya sympathetically.

I nodded, only half-listening. My mind was still focused on . . . Slim. I slumped through all my classes that day, barely paying attention. When the final bell rang at the end of classes, I rushed home, anxious to talk to Baba.

When I got home, Baba was back to sleeping. In fact, he seemed to sleep or sit almost the entire week, until bad news shook us all on Friday.

The wailing and drums began around noon,

coming from beyond the hills down the valley to our home. I felt a chill go through me. A lot of my classmates lived in that direction.

Within half an hour we learned that Supa had died at the hospital.

That weekend little Supa was buried. Baba managed to walk the quarter mile to Abeth's compound for the funeral, though he had to sit down as soon as we arrived.

The main house sat vacant, a sad monument to Abeth's parents. Abeth and Supa had been living in their grandmother's hut. It was a cozy, well-kept little structure. Standing here now with the rest of the mourners, I remembered how Abeth's grandmother had taught Abeth and me how to repair the hut's mud floors and walls by smearing them with a mud mixture. I'd loved it, except the part where we had to collect cow dung and mix it with the dirt. We'd twisted our noses as we worked our feet in the blend. But after smearing it on the floor and smoothing it out, we'd had fun decorating it with pieces of aloe vera leaves. Their prickly edges created patterns as we gently drew the leaves over the wet, sticky floor. By the end of the day, when the floors were dry, the cow dung smell had disappeared. Maybe we had just gotten used to it, but the hut had smelled fresh and clean to us.

The happy memory felt out of place now, like a dream, or a story from someone else's life. Abeth's dani's hut now held as much sadness as the abandoned main house.

During the burial ceremony, Abeth was beside herself. She shed more tears for Supa than she had for her parents. Supa had been the only person left in her family, other than her grandmother.

Baby was bewildered, walking around Abeth's compound, staring at people, trying to understand. I kept her close to me. It wasn't until after Supa was buried deep in the ground that the loss seemed to hit her. She cried and cried.

I wanted to fight something, someone, but I had no idea who or what to blame. Supa had died of malaria. What would I do, go and smash every disease-bearing mosquito that buzzed in Koromo?

Later, when Abeth had calmed down, she whispered to me in a hollow voice, "The hospital doctor who treated Supa said she died partly because of malnutrition. Her body was so weak she couldn't recover from the malaria."

"Abeth, I'm so sorry."

"I failed her, Auma."

"No! It wasn't your fault. What more could you have done for her?"

"I could've dropped out of school and gone to work—earned enough to buy more food . . ."

I wanted to reassure her that she wasn't to blame. But how could I argue with the facts?

Supa died with an empty stomach, at the age of four.

♦♦♦

The day after the funeral I heard Baby whispering softly to one of her corn dolls. "Supa, our friend, is resting. That's what Auma said. I think it's true, but I miss her so much."

She rocked the doll in her arms. "Your new name is Supa. Just don't get sick and die."

While I stood there holding back tears, Baby looked up and saw me watching her. Instantly her face turned angry. "Why are you spying on me?" she shouted, leaping to her feet. "Go away, Auma! Leave me alone!"

"I didn't mean to spy, Baby," I said. "I just— came to bring you some nguru." I took a piece of the sweet out of my pocket and held it out to her. Still glaring at me, she snatched it out of my hand. "I'm proud of you for saying nice things about Supa," I added. "You're a good and brave girl."

She silently stared down at her doll and sucked on her nguru. I left her alone as she'd asked and decided to leave her healing to God.

It took more than a week for Abeth to return to school. She came back in a zombie-like state. Most days she arrived late, her eyes tired and blank. At recess, we sat next to each other in silence. She didn't even wait for me at the gate after school.

If this continued, I thought I just might die, too.

CHAPTER 6

Baba had been home from work in the city for almost a month now. Every day he woke up late and just sat around. One afternoon he got out of his chair to help Mama in the garden, but after plucking about five weeds, he grabbed his stomach and headed back inside. As the days wore on, he grew thinner and he talked less and less. Friends and neighbors came by to see him. Meanwhile Mama earned as much money as she could by selling ropes made from sisal plants and by working for a lady who sold pots at the market. But it wasn't enough, and I worried about what kinds of stories people were concocting about my "lazy" father.

"Mama, is Baba going back to the city soon?"

I asked her this as she and my brothers and I weeded the garden. I kept my voice low, afraid that Baba might overhear me. He was sleeping in the main house, just a few feet away. It was the first time any of us children had brought up Baba's illness. Mama and Dani never mentioned it while we were around, but of course they had all day to talk while we were at school.

Mama pretended she hadn't heard my question. "Hey, why is everyone looking at me?"

"We want to know if Baba is going back to Nairobi," said Juma, backing me up.

"I'm not sure," Mama finally answered, and her voice cracked. "We'll have to wait and see how he fares with the medications from the clinic." She nervously unwrapped her *leso* from her waist and then slowly retied it, letting the cloth wrap cover her ankle. "Just keep praying for him. *Ask and you shall receive*," she quoted, sounding just like Pastor Joseph. "Boys, it's time for you to go get the cattle from the pasture. Hurry up—we'll be eating soon. You all have school tomorrow, so the sooner you go to bed, the better."

Technically, Baby didn't have school yet, and for the rest of us, tomorrow was the last day of the third term before Christmas break. But Mama's message was clear: *Enough questions. Back to work.*

◆◆◆

At suppertime that night my siblings sat wordlessly and waited for Mama and me to bring in the food as we did every night. Our meals had gotten simpler since Baba's return. Without his wages, Mama had to be more careful about her spending. I wished I'd never complained about the smell of the fish I had to carry home from the market. Oh, how I wanted to eat fish right now. Even if it was only a bite. But ugali and sukuma wiki would have to do.

For the past week, Baba hadn't joined us at the table. Instead, he reclined on the sofa with his food on a stool beside him. Dani hadn't been coming to dinner either since Baba came home, and I happily took her food to her hut. Without Dani and Baba at the table, at least I wouldn't have to eat on the floor.

It was Baby who broke the silence at the table. "Mama, can Supa come over and play?" Baby asked, playfully shaping her ugali into a ball. Mama tried ignoring Baby by feeding her, but Baby kept repeating her question.

"I want to have Supa come play." Her voice was sadder this time, as if she was going to cry. I'd thought she had gotten over Supa's death.

"Supa's dead. She's never coming back," Musa said, looking at Baby directly for a moment. He shoveled the rest of his ugali in his mouth and left the table. Mama sighed but didn't call him back. I squeezed Baby's hand, hoping to comfort her.

From the other room, the terrible sound of Baba's cough escalated. Mama went in to see if Baba was all right, and I took Baby onto my lap, where she fell asleep. Mama emerged, supporting Baba on her shoulder. She sat him on his sofa. Juma and Musa watched, their faces practically frozen. Baba's arms were now as thin as Juma's. He'd always been so solid and vigorous. Now, the outlines of his once bulging muscles were only faint ridges. If you hadn't known Baba before, you never would have guessed he had been working hard his entire life.

"Mama Auma, let me know when you're done readying the bedroom," Baba said. I was impressed with how calm his voice was. He didn't want to worry us. Always taking care, making sure we felt protected. That was our Baba.

"All right, just relax for a moment," Mama called out from the bedroom. "Try eating your food while I make the bed. Auma, help your father."

"Baba," I said, "may I bring you some water?"

"Yes, thank you," he responded, closing his eyes and turning his head up.

I hadn't had a normal conversation with Baba, or heard him tease me, in a long time.

I got some freshly boiled drinking water from the pot in the corner of the room. He drank it deeply and handed back the cup.

"Baba, you're going to get well," I said, as much to convince myself as to encourage him.

"Yes, I think so. Today's just been a rough day," he sighed. It was hard to even make small talk with him, let alone ask any delicate questions.

"Hello? Hello?" A woman's voice rang through the window. Who would be stopping by at such an hour?

I opened the back door to discover Mama Karen standing there. She turned her flashlight toward her face so that I could see her better. A shudder went up my spine. What did this loose-lipped woman want so late in the night?

Mama rushed out the door to make sure that Mama Karen wouldn't come inside and see Baba.

"Evening, Jane. I heard Baba Auma was ill, and I wanted to see if there was anything I could do."

"We're just fine, thank you for your kindness," Mama said curtly, without inviting Mama Karen in. This was very unusual for Mama.

"It's just I've never heard of malaria taking such a toll on a grown man for such a long time. I hadn't run into Auma at the market recently, so I thought I'd stop over myself."

Mama Karen hadn't seen me at the market the past few weeks because I avoided her, crouching behind wheelbarrows heaped full of produce and ducking into shops whenever I spotted her.

"He's doing better, Karen, thank you. I was just getting the children to bed. I appreciate you stopping by." Mama led our neighbor to the gate.

"I'll say my prayers to the good Lord for him and your family, Jane."

"Thank you, Karen. Good night."

Mama Karen waited a moment to see if Mama would add anything, and let out a loud sigh as she turned and disappeared into the night, the beam from her flashlight leading the way.

Mama stayed where she was, staring out into the darkness.

By the time she came back inside, I'd helped Baba into bed, settled Baby on her mat, and whisked Juma and Musa out to the kitchen.

With everyone else asleep, I was hoping Mama would confide in me more about Baba's illness. If the rest of the village had heard about it, surely it was time for *us* to talk about it openly.

"Let's go to the choo before we go to bed," I suggested to her, and together we headed to the outhouse.

While Mama was in the choo, I asked, "Mama, what is making Baba so sick?"

"My child, I don't know what it is. I thought he had malaria and typhoid, but it's worse. I'm puzzled by how thin he's growing—and by that cough. He says the doctor only has more questions each time he visits. Tomorrow I'll insist on going with him to the clinic."

From her weary tone, I could tell she wasn't in the mood to say much else. And maybe she didn't actually know any more than I did. The thought of Mama being at a loss was almost as frightening and confusing as the belief that she was purposely keeping me in the dark.

But at least she'd be consulting the doctor tomorrow. We'd know more soon.

Back in the house, I tiptoed into the sitting room, curled up close to Baby, and fell asleep to the innocent sound of her light snore.

CHAPTER 7

The next morning Mama woke up very early to take Baba to the clinic. My siblings and I woke to find porridge already cooked for us. Mama gave me clear instructions about chores for everyone, in case she wasn't back by the afternoon.

"Mama Auma," I could hear Baba calling from the bedroom. "Why don't you stay and take care of the children? I can take myself to the doctor."

Mama frowned. "If you can get up by yourself, get water from the pot outside, carry it to the reed washroom, take a bath, and then walk two miles to the bus stop, then I won't go with you to the doctor. Otherwise, I'm coming."

Baba, Mama, and Dani were the only ones in the family who regularly used the reed washroom. The rest of us usually bathed in the stream so that we wouldn't have to carry home extra water for washing. Baba had said over and over how he was going to put real walls around the reed washroom, just like the city bathrooms he'd gotten used to. It sounded nice, but I still thought I'd prefer to bathe in the Haha, where the water was cold and refreshing and I could use as much water as I wanted.

At this point, I couldn't imagine my father making it all the way to the stream to bathe.

Baba staggered into the sitting room and collapsed onto the sofa. From his drawn expression, it was clear he was not going to the doctor on his own.

Baba let Mama put his arm over her neck as he slowly walked with her across the compound yard and through the gate. They moved like slugs. I probably could have run back and forth fifteen times in the amount of time it took Mama to drag Baba with her to the bus stop.

With Mama gone, I was in charge of pretty much everything. I turned back to the tasks at hand. First Juma and Musa had to take the cattle out to the pasture. Meanwhile I had to get Baby dressed and breakfast on the table.

"Do we have to go to school?" Musa moaned

when he and Juma came back in. "It's almost the end of term anyway . . ."

"Then you can handle one more day," I said sternly. My brothers were looking forward to the break, but I would miss school. And not just because I loved reading and science and math. School was a place where things were written down. Classes ran on a predictable schedule. Unlike our home now, you knew what to expect.

"I'm so sick of porridge," Baby whined, and Juma and Musa chimed in.

"Auma, aren't there any bananas?" Juma asked halfheartedly, already knowing the answer.

At this point, I wanted to scream at everybody. "Eat what's in front of you," I said in my firmest voice.

These days, porridge was all we would eat in the morning. Like Juma, I wished we could have bananas or boiled cassava or potatoes. But now Baba had no income, so Mama's market list shrank every week. I no longer found it fun to visit the market. The sweet aroma of cooked chicken made me want to beg for food.

As we slurped our porridge, I remembered a story Dani had told us when we were younger. "Story come," she would always say before she started, and we would call back, "Story come."

"Once upon a time there was a drought in the forest and all the animals had to carefully ration the little food they had. Mr. Hare finished almost all his food first. With only a little flour left for ugali, he decided to beg for food. Mr. Elephant was cooking some great-smelling dish. So Mr. Hare cooked the little ugali and walked over to Mr. Elephant's house."

Dani would ask in a small voice, *"Hey, my friend elephant, can you share your food with me?"*

Then her voice turned deep and heavy like Baba's. "*No, I am sorry*, Mr. Elephant immediately replied." She would pause as we giggled uncontrollably.

"*Please, please*, begged Mr. Hare, but Mr. Elephant refused. So Mr. Hare said, *Okay, let me sit outside here. I will eat my ugali, along with the aroma from your food.*"

"*Fine, suit yourself*, Mr. Elephant responded. With that, Mr. Elephant dipped his trunk into his plate and lifted it into his mouth. Since he was big he could not see his plate as he put his trunk into his mouth. Mr. Hare helped himself to Mr. Elephant's food each time Mr. Elephant put his trunk into his mouth. When Mr. Hare's ugali was done, he thanked the elephant for sharing the aroma of his food and walked away." At the end of the story, Dani would say, "Don't steal other people's things, not even an aroma."

It had been an amusing story back when we were little, but now I sympathized with Mr. Hare.

Even though I wasn't too sure about our new-found faith in Jesus, I prayed to Him as I ran to school. I prayed that Jesus would heal Baba. That we would eat fish again and that our family would laugh again.

I picked up my pace. The cold wind blowing past my head made me feel as if my worries were flying away from me like leaves on a windy day. I could think clearly again. I felt energized, as if I'd just had a race with fear and won.

For now.

♦♦♦

That evening when Mama and Baba returned home from the clinic, Mama looked like she had seen Death himself. Her eyes wandered over the things in our house, resting on them blankly.

"Mama, did you get some new medication from the doctor?" was all I dared ask.

"Yes," she answered in a faraway voice, and stared at me as if she was looking through me. She didn't even help Baba into his chair before slouching down into her own, her head in her hands.

Baba, I noticed, looked worse than ever. His pants hung looser, and he walked unsteadily, like a wobbly deflated tire. Whatever they were processing, I sensed now was not the time to badger them with more questions.

◆◆◆

"Something is wrong with my father," I blurted out to Abeth a few days later, as we walked home from Haha with our freshly washed laundry. Our feet slapped the ground in rhythm, sending soft clouds of dust behind us as we walked on. A crowned crane flying overhead broke the silence with its loud cry piercing the breeze around us. I waited for it to pass before I continued.

"He spends most of his days in bed. He has all these medications that he takes every day, but Mama has to help him with everything—relieving himself, bathing, even eating when he feels up to it." And since their visit to the clinic, Mama had been like a robot. She went through all the motions of taking care of Baba, but stopped encouraging him to do anything, and she didn't joke with him anymore. "I don't think he's ever going back to the city."

Abeth turned and touched my arm gently. "Do you think that all of Koromo doesn't know your father is sick, Auma? I've known for a while."

I felt stupid for thinking I could keep anything from Abeth, and ashamed that I had tried. But she'd been so wrapped up in grief for Supa that I hadn't wanted to add to her worries.

"You know, there's talk about an evil spirit that's invading the village," Abeth said. "Your father should see the medicine man right away. He'll know what to do."

I stared at Abeth. She was completely serious.

"Stop it, Abeth!" I snapped. "Why do you talk like that? Our family doesn't believe in that kind of healing anymore, remember?"

"I know, but my grandmother said that the new disease in Koromo can't be healed with modern medicine."

I gritted my teeth in frustration. Clearly Abeth was forgetting how much I wanted to be a doctor. If it was a choice between modern medicine and the medicine man's vague methods, my instinct was to trust modern medicine. "If the medicine man's treatments truly work, why isn't everyone in Koromo consulting him?"

"Because they're like you—too afraid of what they don't understand."

"I'm not afraid!" I cried indignantly. But . . . was that the truth? I cast about for the easiest way to end the argument. "I just think we should pray to God to heal the sick, like Pastor Joseph said at church."

"All right, you pray to God for your father's healing," Abeth sighed, giving in. She made a waving motion across her forehead to indicate she was willing to drop the subject. But I knew she hadn't put much faith in God since her parents' deaths. If I'd lost my whole family, I'd probably question God, too.

For a moment, we were quiet, walking and looking straight ahead, buckets balanced on our heads, as though we were waiting for answers way ahead where the road ended and our sight grew cloudy.

Abeth bit her lip. "You know, Auma—it may not be an evil spirit, but something is really wrong. Everyone is dying, old and young. I thought I had to wait until old age to die, but . . ." She broke off, then took a deep breath. "Look, my parents died young," she said, still looking ahead. "And I think they should have tried different ways, every way, to get well. They never tried going to the medicine man. Maybe if they had, they'd still be here."

I knew how hard it was for Abeth to talk about her parents. I listened quietly, knowing how much courage it must take for her to say this to me.

"Maybe if they—had lasted longer—Supa would've been able to remember them better. And maybe, if my parents had had more time to provide for us, Supa herself . . . would still be alive."

"Oh, Abeth," I murmured. The thought of poor Supa, her body weakened by malnourishment, was like a stone in my stomach.

Abeth turned to me and managed to smile. "You know, Auma, I wasn't sure I would make it. But I think, in spite of everything, I'm all right now. I can let the past be. It's the future that concerns me. You're going to need someone, and I want to be there for you. You were there for me."

"Thank you," I said.

Maybe she was right. Maybe family was worth trying everything for.

It would go against all Mama's beliefs, but if Baba got any worse, I wondered if she'd consider testing the power of the medicine man.

♦♦♦

Swish, swish, swish. I awoke to a rubbing sound, coming from the wall near my head. My body froze as I tried to figure out what it was. The sun was already up, but no one was awake. Suddenly I remembered— it was Christmas Day.

I crawled off my mattress toward the window, unlatched it, and peeked outside, only to see the smooth behind of a cow. The cows were out!

"Juma, Musa!" I yelled. "The cows are out! Get them before they leave the compound!"

Soon the compound was busy with running feet and the sounds of clicking tongues, as the boys rounded up the cows and put them back into the boma. Baby and I sat on the veranda to watch, not bothering to help, for the boys were good at getting the cows together. Peace returned by the time the adults joined us.

Christmas was a special time in Koromo, for Christians and non-Christians alike. Very early in the morning, most Christians went to church. Some had new clothes while others wore their best church outfits. Afterward, people returned home to prepare the Christmas meal of meats, rice, and *chapati*, flat bread. In the afternoon, families would treat their children to candy at the shopping center. Others stayed home, the children playing together while the adults visited with their relatives or guests.

Back when Baba was well, Christmas was the best day of the year. Baba always invited relatives and neighbor friends to join us for the Christmas meal. There was plenty to eat: beef, chicken, ugali, bread, and soda. Baba bought new clothes for us from the city. He would give us money to buy sweets. He let us, with a whole bunch of our cousins, go to the shopping center without adult supervision. Back home we would play till we could play no longer.

At night, the village would come alive with the sound of boom boxes playing music from all corners of the countryside, near and far. The night parties would go on till dawn, but before we went to sleep we would sit outside in the warm night under the sky and just talk quietly, half listening to the music, as Mama told stories of her past Christmastimes. Most were so funny we laughed until our bellies hurt.

I walked into the kitchen to find Mama mixing flour.

"Mama, we are going to have chapati? When did you buy the flour? May I help? What will we have with them?" I could not stop asking questions.

Mama smiled. "Okay, young lady, calm down. I will use your help very soon. Get your brothers to help you catch the red hen."

I didn't wait for the rest of the instructions. I ran out, calling to Musa and Juma to catch the hen. We always enjoyed chasing chickens and catching them, even though most of the time we caught them for sale and not for us to eat. I could practically smell the aroma of cooked chicken already.

We started by surrounding the hen, arms stretched out to block the space between us. As we slowly closed in like a pack of hyenas, the hen saw us approaching and ran for the gap between Musa and Juma. Musa reached out but missed, and the chase began. Chickens and feathers and squeals flew in all directions. All over the compound the chase continued until the hen finally tired and began to slow down. Baby cheered on from the veranda, and the hen made one last attempt to escape, leaping up in the air. Juma caught her mid-flight, like a goalkeeper catching a ball, and we all cheered at his skill.

Mama quickly slaughtered the hen, and the three of us plucked the feathers. While Mama cooked chapatis, I cut up the chicken under Dani's supervision. "It's high time you learned how to make a good chicken stew," Dani said briskly. I decided not to tell her that it wasn't easy to remember how to cook certain dishes when we could afford so little food.

"Go wash the pieces and bring the pot, so we can boil the chicken first."

It was unusual for Dani to take such a lead in our kitchen when Mama was there. I supposed this Christmas brought the spirit of togetherness and joy in a different way.

"You're doing fine," Dani told me once I had the chicken in the pot. "Keep an eye on the water while I go pick some herbs for your father in the garden."

My grandmother knew about herbs for almost every kind of illness, even some that didn't grow locally. I drew a deep breath and ventured, "Dani, the medicine man uses herbs to cure people, right? Can you use your herbs to heal Baba?"

Her stern old face seemed to lose some of its hardness as she shook her head. "My child, this thing that your father has is beyond herbs. There are too many things happening in his weak body. My herbs can only handle one sickness at a time. Only God can cure something like this."

"Then why give him any herbs at all, Dani?" I hoped I hadn't offended her.

Dani frowned. "Auma. Who gave us these herbs?"

"You did," I responded, confused.

"Who gave me the seeds? The knowledge? The rain to make them grow? Who gave my ancestors all of that?" I understood what Dani was saying— that there was no other choice but to trust in God for Baba's healing. Pastor Joseph said the same kinds of things during his sermons: *Do not give up when you feel that God is far away,* and *With God, all things are possible.*

I felt a tinge of anger. If it were possible for God to cure Baba, why didn't He?

◆◆◆

Around noon our neighbors the Bimas stopped by to visit. Mr. Bima had worked in a high government position before he retired, so he and his wife, Mama Benta, lived in one of the nicest houses in the village. I'd heard many people in Koromo grumble about the Bimas, saying they were selfish and thought they were better than the rest of us. But Mama had been casual friends with Mama Benta for a long time, and I'd never heard either of the Bimas say anything unkind.

Baba was now settled under the jwelu tree near the kitchen, comfortably propped up with a rolled-up blanket.

"Baba Auma, I see you're gaining strength now," said Mr. Bima.

"Yes, yes, my friend." Baba nodded. "Christmas has something to do with it." I sensed a hint of joy in his voice. He asked about the Bimas' daughter, Amina, who lived in Nairobi, and the Bimas shared the latest news from the city before they moved on to visit other families. I wondered if Baba missed Nairobi, with its daily surprises and challenges, so different from the stagnant life he'd been living lately. But maybe there was still a chance he'd get well enough to go back there for work . . .

By two o'clock we filed into the house, ready to eat. I was happy we hadn't invited others to our dinner. We were so hungry for food, any food. Mama prayed over the full table, especially thankful for

Baba's health. But just as we started to eat, a loud voice interrupted our meal.

"Hallo! Is anyone home?" Mama Karen's voice rang through the door.

"Come in," Mama called out. "Help yourself to some chicken and chapati."

"Merry Christmas to all of you," she greeted us, raising her hands up the way priests do to bless people. With our mouths filled with chapati and chicken, we responded in unison, "Merry Christmas."

Mama Karen ate heartily and talked even more heartily. "I heard your niece Tabitha turned down a marriage proposal! Can you imagine? All on her own with that child to support, and only her mother-in-law to help her with the farming—and she slams the door in some poor man's face . . ."

"My dear, how do you know such information?" Mama cut in. Even we, Tabitha's relatives, hadn't heard about this.

Mama Karen laughed in her rough voice. "Remember, working at the market allows me to listen and talk to people from all around and beyond this village. Come to think of it, I get morning news before the newspaper gets to our market." Everyone chuckled politely.

At least she had good humor about her gossip habit. I just hoped she wasn't spreading lies, especially where Tabitha was concerned. I could hardly believe my cousin had refused a marriage proposal, but if she had—good for her! She shouldn't have to take another husband just because it was expected of her.

After the meal, everyone's spirits seemed lifted. Juma, Musa, and Baby went out to play as the adults talked. Baba was too tired to stay up, so Mama helped him to his room. But they both seemed more relaxed, more comfortable with each other—*happier*—than they had in weeks. And I saw the calmness on Baba's face and hoped that Christmas had begun some sort of healing.

CHAPTER 8

January arrived with its rains and its new school term. I was now in Class Eight.

The excitement of being one class higher seemed to have infected almost everyone. And my spirits were feeling especially light thanks to the slight improvement in Baba. Just maybe Baba was going to get well.

To prepare for the upcoming national exams, those in Class Eight were expected to be at school no later than six in the morning, two hours before school started. I didn't mind at all. Most of us couldn't do much deep studying at home. Many of our homes had poor lighting, and it was hard to stay focused when we were surrounded by family members and chores. During morning study time at school, we had a bright lantern and plenty of quiet space. I loved being able to concentrate on learning—loved being one step closer to high school.

◆◆◆

One day, nearly all the Class Seven boys were late getting back to class after recess. They'd been lost in their game of soccer and hadn't heard the bell. After school, the boys were ordered to sweep the school compound yard—a girl's chore—as punishment.

While the boys worked, Magi placed her hands on her curvy hips and called the other girls over to plot something. I didn't feel like joining them, and Abeth and I hung back, resting for a moment before heading home. Suddenly the huddle broke as Magi swooshed around and yelled, "Hey, we would like to see which boy is brave enough to talk to the tough Auma Onyango!"

All the other girls joined in with a loud "Yes, yes!"

"Why would they choose me?" I whispered to Abeth.

"Because you're always so sharp and serious whenever boys are around," she murmured back. "They want the boys to have a challenge."

"Magi," I shot back, "tell me if you know any

boy who will climb trees and go to the stream and collect firewood with me. Let me know if there's a boy who would do my chores for me if I was sick, without complaining. I will have that boy as my boyfriend."

I couldn't even believe I'd said the word *boyfriend*. My neighbor Sussie had always said that once you had a boyfriend, you had to sleep with him to confirm your commitment to him. I wasn't sure why it had to happen. But I knew Mama would kill me if she even *suspected* me of fooling around with any boy.

"Let's wait and see," Magi answered. "One will try to talk to you soon, and I want to be there to see it."

"Look!" said Teresa, jumping up and down with delight. "Abuya is coming for you, Auma!"

I looked up and my heart began to race. If it were anyone but Abuya, deciding what to do would have been easier. Abuya was the only boy who asked me how Abeth was doing when she wasn't at school, and asked if I was doing all right. In a way, he wasn't as boyish as the others. He was more thoughtful, more considerate. Like Baba.

I realized in that moment that I'd left my composition book inside the classroom and darted back inside to get it, pretending I hadn't seen him heading my way. When I returned to the door, Abuya blocked my path.

"You can't leave," he said, his eyes looking right into mine. I made the terrible, terrible mistake of looking right back into his eyes. I thought my chest would burst open. He looked so nervous and so determined at the same time, and underneath all that I still saw a hint of his usual gentleness.

"I need to go home, Abuya. Let me pass," I managed to say.

He stood before me with his chest thrust out and his feet planted squarely in the doorway. What did he think he was proving? Didn't he know I had liked him precisely because he *didn't* act tough and manly? "Auma, I've tried to make friends with you for a long time, and you don't even want to talk to me. Today, will you please talk to me, Auma?"

Abeth called out, "Abuya, that's enough! Stop bothering Auma!"

She had no idea how I felt about Abuya.

By now a group of other Class Eight students were huddled outside, watching and listening. "Auma, just be his girlfriend. We know you want to!" Magi shouted.

"Say you'll be my girlfriend and I'll move out of the way," Abuya said, moving toward me while the other kids laughed. He moved close enough that I could smell his sweat.

My resolve returned. With all the force I could muster, I pushed him out of my way.

And then I took off running.

Abuya came after me. I realized that if I didn't drop my heavy book bag, he was going to catch me. I flung it down as I dashed toward the gate. I could hear Abuya panting at my heels, so I turned and ran straight into the crowd of students. I zigzagged between them, hoping Abuya would give up, but he kept up with my speed. With track season not yet started and with the busy life at home, I was out of practice.

Part of me was screaming that I should stop and just let him catch up to me. But I didn't. I kept on winding back and forth as students from other classes stopped to watch. Some thought we were just playing a game, so they began to cheer.

"Auma, Auma!" they chanted.

Most of the boys were taunting Abuya, rather than cheering him on.

"Man, if you don't catch that girl you're chicken. Catch her!" they yelled.

I knew that to save my reputation, and maybe even my dignity, I had to outrun him. I left the crowd and made for the gate that led to the shopping center. I realized that if I kept going straight, I would end up in the middle of the shopping center parking lot, and I could easily get hit by a speeding car.

Abruptly, I circled a massive tree that was growing out of a rise in the road and dashed back toward the school gate. I flew down the steep slope as fast as lightning, distancing myself nicely from Abuya. I checked over my shoulder and it seemed he was slowing down. I was smiling at my luck when *wham!*

The ground rushed up to my face, and I found myself spitting out a mouthful of dirt. I heard a group of girls rushing toward me, calling out, but my vision was blurred.

"Auma, are you okay? Let us help you get up."

I shook my head to clear my vision, only to see a huge cloud of dust settling, as if there had been an explosion. I nodded and extended my arms to let them lift me up. As I winced, crystals of dirt gritted between my teeth. My dress and skin were caked in dirt, like a traditional dancer painted for a funeral ceremony.

"You're bleeding!" somebody exclaimed.

It was Abeth. She arrived as the other girls were helping me to my feet. My book bag was slung over her shoulder. She must've stopped to pick it up after I dropped it.

I was out of breath but tried my best to sound normal. My heart was pounding in my throat like the sound of the funeral drums, steadily beating every time another death was announced in Koromo.

"Blood on your knee, your elbow . . . and here on your shoulder," Abeth said as she checked me all over. That's when she saw a spot of blood on my dress and gasped. I figured I had been cut down there, too, although I couldn't feel any specific pain. My entire body ached.

I held onto Abeth to support my trembling body. I was hurting so badly that I thought I was going to collapse.

"I will be fine," I lied.

"Let's get you home," said Abeth.

"Where's Abuya?" I asked, holding onto Abeth's shoulder as I limped. Anger welled up in my chest. This was all his fault.

"He walked that way," she said, pointing toward a small path near the side of the school compound. "Don't even worry about him." Abeth glanced at my dress again, with a worried look. "Let's get out of here," she said.

Most of the students had seen the race, and they'd also seen me fall. They gave way as I limped past them. Some were asking exactly what happened. Others expressed their sympathy: "Mos, mos."

I whispered, so no one could hear, "I don't know how I'll make it home, Abeth!" Holding onto Abeth's shoulder, I began to cry. My body ached. But more than that: I had made a fool of myself in front of the whole school, and my embarrassment was worse than the wounds on my knees.

Eventually we stopped at a small pond that had formed after the rains. Abeth sat me down on a huge rock that stuck up out of the edge of the pond. She reached for a soft hairy leaf and used it to wipe my wounds. "This will soothe the pain and slow the bleeding."

She squeezed the leaf until it was bruised. She dipped it in the water and wiped my knee and elbow as I continued to cry.

"Thanks," I said, wiping away my tears. "It feels better."

"There, get up, let's go home." As she helped me hobble along, she asked, "Why did you run?"

More tears welled up in my eyes. "Abeth, I will not be anyone's girlfriend. Don't you see he was forcing me?"

"You know Auma, if I were you, I would've faced him and told him to stop harassing me. I would've warned him that I was going to tell my parents if he ever talked to me again."

I didn't know how to explain the mixed-up feelings that had made me run. As much as I'd hated the situation Abuya put me in, I also couldn't forget the way Abuya made me feel when he showed me kindness.

Instead I said, "But I couldn't have actually told my parents. Mama would whip me if she knew how close Abuya got. She might even think I did something to encourage his behavior."

Maybe I had.

I clenched my fists at the thought. Even if he had reason to suspect I really did like him, he still should've seen how upset I was and left me alone when I asked him to.

To my relief, when we reached home, I didn't have to explain my fall to my mother. She and Baba weren't back from the hospital yet. Abeth made sure Musa and Juma headed to the kitchen to start the fire. Then she quickly ushered me into the house.

"Auma, did you know that you're bleeding?"

"Isn't that obvious?" I snapped. "I fell flat on my face, Abeth."

"No. I mean you're *bleeding*," Abeth whispered, so that the boys out back couldn't hear. She pointed to the front of my dress.

"Oh my!" I panicked. My womanhood was here.

"Well, it's about time you started going to the moon. You're way past the usual starting age."

I hadn't even realized that Abeth was already "going to the moon," as we called it. Periods were private business. If the boys found out that a girl was on her period, they'd tease her mercilessly.

Abeth found a piece of an old pillowcase for me to wrap around my waist. Then she sent me to the choo with the little bit of water that was left from Baba's morning bath. Abeth made sure Juma, Musa, and Baby stayed away while I washed, changed my clothes, and stuffed the cloth in my underwear. I'd learned about menstruation in school, but still had so many questions. As soon as Mama got home, I would ask her . . .

Then I stiffened. If I told Mama, then she'd tell

Dani. My grandmother was already irritating me with her comments on how I was growing to be a hardworking woman. If she knew this had happened, she'd burden me with even more talk of marriage.

No, I wouldn't tell. I'd hide it. And I wouldn't miss school like the other girls did when they were having their periods. I'd steal one of Baby's old thick blankets and cut it into strips that would absorb the blood. At lunchtime, I could use the school choos to change it. No one would know.

The pain in my elbow shot up, and I bit my lip. *Don't cry*, I thought. *You're a woman now.*

Which made me want to cry even more.

It seemed as if adulthood had always been lurking around the corner, and today it had caught up with me. One minute it's my normal responsibilities, the next it's womanhood.

If Dani had her way, I'd quit school now and leave home to get married. Leave my parents and siblings behind. Leave Abeth and all our friends . . .

Then I thought of Abuya again. Thought of how school, my safe haven, had suddenly turned into a threatening place where I was cornered—where I didn't know whom to trust.

Did I really want to spend my life in Koromo?

I gritted my teeth. *Only if I can become a doctor. Then I can return and treat the sick. I can change people's lives for the better.*

But I wouldn't become just another woman, to be chased around and married off. I would be Auma, the child born facedown, who refused to give up and confounded everyone's expectations.

I limped back into the house, feeling the cloth in my underwear slide back and forth. Great. I had a lifetime of pillowcases and blanket strips to look forward to.

And I had no idea what I would say to Abuya the next time I saw him.

CHAPTER 9

One afternoon, as I looked at Baba, a silent fear gripped my heart. Whatever strength Baba had seemed to regain over Christmas was long gone. He spent every day in bed, he barely ate, and his cough was worse. Everyone had completely stopped talking about his illness. Even Baby stopped asking when Baba was going to get better so he could swing her around and around.

I wanted to talk.

Even if no one had the answers, I wanted to ask a million questions. And I wanted to ask them out loud. Why couldn't we talk about it?

"Mama, how is Baba doing? Is he getting better?"

Mama sighed. "I wish I could say that he was. I've been praying for him ever since he came home, but it hasn't helped."

"Mama . . . couldn't we go to the medicine man?" I blurted out.

Her jaw dropped. "What did you just say?"

I squared my shoulders and looked her in the eye. "We could try the medicine man. What do we have to lose?"

"Auma!" She looked at me as if she didn't recognize me. "We're Christians now. I thought you understood that the medicine man is against our faith."

Faith hasn't saved Baba, I thought furiously. Aloud I said, "I don't believe that bad spirits are causing Baba's illness, Mama, but isn't it still possible that the medicine man could help? Isn't it worthwhile to at least talk to him?"

Mama sniffed and turned from the smoky fire. "The medicine man is not the answer. Jesus is the only answer."

This was more than I could take. My stomach felt sick. I stood up and slowly walked away.

"Auma? Where are you going?"

Away, I thought. *Have to get away from here.*

"I'm just going to the stream for some extra water before it gets dark."

Before she could caution me about going to the stream alone, I grabbed our plastic bucket and ran.

As I neared the stream, I overheard Mama Karen and Nyar Kano talking. They didn't see me approaching, but as I walked slowly toward them, I could clearly hear their voices.

"Simu has been home sick for three months now." When I heard my father's name, I stopped and hid myself behind a thorny bush.

"What's the matter with him?"

"My dear, nowadays do you even need to ask? When you see somebody who left Koromo healthy and comes back home from the city sick, you know what it is."

My stomach clenched. Over and over again I'd asked myself what could possibly be wrong with Baba. Over and over again I came up with only one answer. And yet I'd kept hoping that I was wrong. That Mama would have some other explanation for me.

"Are you sure?"

"Ah, my dear, you only have to look at his size to confirm it. The modern disease doesn't spare anyone, especially those who work in the city."

"But that means Simu would have had to . . ."

At this point, I emerged from my hiding place, interrupting her mid-sentence. I couldn't bear to hear any more. Besides, I was a woman now, just like them. I didn't have to hide behind a bush like a child.

"Eh, Auma, how is your mother doing?" Mama Karen asked.

"Fine," I replied coldly, without even looking her way.

"I heard your father is still home from the city. It's been some months now, right? How is he doing?" she pushed.

"He'll be touched that you're so concerned," I said, not even caring how rude I sounded. Then I squatted down and started to fill my pail with water, which was more difficult than usual because water wasn't as plentiful in the dry season. It seemed Koromo was running out of everything good these days.

The two women fell silent, probably shocked by my lack of manners. *Let them be shocked*, I thought bitterly. *I've asked enough questions without getting an answer. Well, I have a right to keep my answers to myself too.* At least I could be in control of something—my thoughts and words.

CHAPTER 10

A few days later I came home from school to find Mama crouched on the veranda staring into space. Shouldn't she be trying to get Baba to eat? Or Baby? My heart started pounding, as if I had just run a 200-meter dash. I hurried toward Mama, practically throwing my book bag down.

"Mama, Mama, what is it?" I found myself shaking her shoulder, as if to wake her.

Mama didn't utter a word. She just stared straight ahead.

As I looked past her through the open door into our semi-dark hut, I noticed several people in the house. I wondered what all those people were doing in there.

Then I heard my uncle talking. "Let him rest. There isn't much we can do now."

I hurried inside, and my eyes fell upon a form on the dirt floor. It was Baba. Suddenly my feet felt like lead. I stood there and stared at my father. He wasn't moving.

I slowly turned and dragged my heavy feet back toward the door. I staggered like a drunk old man. I knew what death was, but then again, I didn't.

Out on the veranda, I quietly sat down next to Mama. Maybe she would make things better.

I whispered, "Mama, we can still take Baba to the medicine man."

"No, my child," Mama whispered back, hushing me. "It's too late for that."

We sat in silence for what seemed like hours. My stomach rumbled, and there was no supper to fill it.

When my uncle emerged from the house, he gently said, "He is gone to rest."

My mother didn't flinch. She stood frozen for an entire minute.

And then she suddenly burst into tears. "Oooh my! What will I do? What will I do?" she screamed.

I knew no neighbor in Koromo would sleep that night.

Mama got up and hustled toward the gate. I hadn't seen her with that much fire in her in months.

Her ululation was the crazed dirge of grief, but it was also a conscious message. It was the call to the village to let people know that a death had occurred in our home.

Mama's cry pierced the darkness, dousing all beauty beneath the starlit sky. The stars were dimmer, the crickets quieter. Other than Mama's terrible screaming, Koromo seemed lifeless.

It was then I felt the permanence of death. Baba was really gone. Forever.

All I wanted to do was crawl in a well and sink to the bottom. But that was the child inside me speaking. I was a woman now. I felt energy flowing back into me. Slowly and with purpose, I took my place next to Mama. I echoed her loud scream and cried, "Baba, Baba, why did you leave us?"

When Mama ran back toward the house, I ran toward the gate. We passed each other, not looking. We didn't need to. We were wrapped up in our shared agony, and we were finally able to voice everything out loud. As we rushed back and forth from the house to the gate, Dani joined us. Dani was too old to do any running, but she hobbled up and down, her walking stick in hand, weeping and talking quietly to herself.

I had never fully understood our tradition—why women wailed so loudly and for so long after someone died. It was only now I realized that women wailed more on account of everything they never had the chance to say. All the questions they never asked. All the times we never really talked about the things that mattered most.

It was the one time that women could be angry. Be loud. Say anything. Yell. Purge the soul. And no one thought less of them. Everyone expected it.

It felt good to let out all of the silt that had settled inside me, even though I knew it wouldn't bring Baba back.

Finally Mama and I were both worn out. We walked back to the house, still quietly weeping. At the door, Dani joined us and all three of us held onto each other, until Dani pulled away and hobbled over to a chair outside her hut. When I sat down on our veranda, I noticed that Juma and Musa had stood outside the house the whole time. I realized, perhaps for the first time, how tall they had grown, and as they wept, they looked like grown men crying. Most of the men sat silently, their faces looking mummi-fied. I had seen some men cry during Abeth's parents' funerals. I guessed those were the weak ones, because men were not supposed to cry. Or were they the strong ones? I wanted everyone to cry, however odd it looked.

Some neighbors had come over to help. The Bimas—Mama Benta and her husband—were the first to arrive. I wondered if Baba's death made them worry about their daughter, so far away from home, in a city that bred horrible nameless diseases.

Tabitha came and stood next to the boys, holding Baby, who was now sleeping. She was still on her own, trying to survive by doing odd jobs around the village and helping her mother-in-law grow peanuts on her small plot of land. I felt a flash of sympathy for her. Our grief must remind her of her own aloneness.

The dried tears had left soft lines on Baby's cheeks that reflected the lantern. I bent down and touched her forehead, and she slowly opened her eyes for a moment before submitting once again to their heaviness.

Mama stood. She couldn't be consoled, and she continued to weep. She paced back and forth at a snail's pace.

"What will I do . . . ," she whispered, her face angled up toward the bright moon that had now risen to its peak in the late night sky. "Why didn't you warn me, my love? Your children deserve better than what lies ahead . . ."

Several hours passed. Mama kept walking and talking to herself. I strained to hear every word that fell from her trembling lips. She whispered to herself their life story, about how she had come to Koromo just because of Baba. How he was the most handsome man she'd ever met, with the smoothest skin and the strongest arms. How he had come back from the city to rest and get well, but he had returned with a monster inside.

But still, I wondered if there was something more that Mama never whispered. She had given up on Baba getting well. In his last days, she seemed to have lost all hope. That wasn't the Mama I knew.

At some point, Mama Benta put her arms around Mama and told her to sit down and rest. Mama lashed her arms, flinging them left and right.

"Why do you tell me to sit down? Don't you want me to mourn my husband?"

Mama Benta was a tall, heavyset woman in her late fifties. She was a lot stronger than Dani, but she couldn't hold on to Mama.

Finally, Mama Karen came over to stand in silence next to Mama, just like I had for Abeth and

Abeth had for me. She whispered, "Jane, please sit down."

I was surprised at her kindness. I could see that she cared for Mama more than I could have imagined.

Mama lifted her head, revealing swollen eyes. She stared into space, as if she was in a trance. She looked like an antelope that had just seen a lion ready to pounce.

"Please rest," Mama Karen said gently.

Before Mama could walk away, Mama Karen took her by the hand, wrapped her arm around her, and led her to the bedroom. There, Mama began wailing again. At last, after hours of consolation and prayers, she drifted into a deep sleep.

The women and children went to bed sometime after one in the morning. Most of the men stayed up all night. They would stay up many more nights, until after the burial.

Tomorrow would be a busy day for everyone. Baba's body would be taken to the mortuary, where it would stay until burial, probably a week later. The length of time would depend on how long it took to collect the money to cover the funeral costs: the price of a coffin, burial clothes, and food for all our guests. I wasn't sure if Mama planned a traditional

Luo burial for Baba, here at home, or if everything would be according to Christian traditions. Maybe Mama never planned anything at all. How could any human being plan ahead for something like this? I too needed to rest like Mama, only I had the feeling that the sun would be up before I could manage to fall asleep.

I laid my mat outside on the veranda near Musa and Juma, where I could see the myriad stars, and began counting. One . . . two . . . three . . . four . . .

CHAPTER 11

Over the next few days, relatives and friends came to mourn Baba. The women joined Mama in screaming and moaning, running up and down the front yard, until Mama was so weak from mourning and fasting that she could barely walk. Once she'd exhausted herself, several women sat with her constantly, singing songs about God and offering words of spiritual comfort. And although Mama nodded as she listened, she didn't sing a word.

My uncles talked about how Baba was a good, honest, hardworking man. They recalled stories of how Baba had lent them money and how he always kept his word. Their voices sounded rich and full, and they reminded me how proud I had been to be a Nyar Simu, Baba's daughter.

I had known my father was a great man, but as

people continued to stream through the gate, even during the middle of the week, anyone who looked around couldn't dispute my father's impact. Since getting a job in the city, Baba had contributed to the village fund-raising efforts. And Mama's work with the women's group had helped dozens of families afford their children's tuition. These women and their families knew that although we didn't have much, we shared what we had. I felt guilty for wishing my mother had been more selfish with our money. My parents' work had made a difference to all these people who had trekked miles to pay their respects.

By Thursday night some of our relatives had helped us construct a temporary shed, where the additional visitors who would arrive on the weekend could assemble. People continued singing songs of consolation and telling stories about Baba as they knew him, or anything relevant to his life. Sometimes, somebody from the crowd would just get up and start preaching, shouting out Bible verses.

A group of people from the local church had brought drums that they played late into the night, long after the singing, preaching, and testimonies were over. Young people danced to the drums until they were exhausted. That night Musa, Juma, and Baby had more life in them than I had seen in months. They danced as if Baba's funeral was a party, a feast. When I was about to question why the children should be allowed to stay up so late dancing, I bit my tongue. Baba had only been gone a couple of days and already I was thinking like the head of the household. I decided to ease up on the reins for now and let my siblings dance. With all the death around us, I certainly didn't want to pour water over a living flame inside anyone.

On Saturday, the day before burial, even more people flooded the yard. I began to wonder where we were going to get enough food to feed them all. Then wondering turned to worrying. What would we eat after the funeral?

I knew how Abeth, Supa, and their grandmother had suffered after her parents were buried. They'd been left without as much as a hen. And then poor Supa had more or less starved . . .

Since I wasn't sure we were going to have food after the burial, I made my brothers and sister eat everything they were served. I'd never known Baby to actually finish her entire plate, but she licked it clean that week. While Mama wasn't on Mama Duty, somebody had to be.

Late on Saturday night, after the drums no longer beat, Mama sent me to the kitchen for a knife so she could cut a piece of fruit. Since I wasn't used to being out that late, I got Juma to take the flashlight and go with me. I could hear people talking in lowered voices in the gloomy darkness. Music played softly from a record player.

"Watch where you step," I whispered to Juma, lunging over one of our cousins. "There are people asleep all over the grass."

"Why can't they go home and sleep?" Juma whispered as we picked our way over to the kitchen.

"I guess they like it here," I said.

"Like it here? Why?" He sounded puzzled.

"Can't you see all the free food?" Some bitterness crept into my voice. "For sure, we won't have anything left for ourselves." Still, part of me knew that our culture encouraged mourning as a community. In that sense, we were getting the support that we needed.

But the community would not be able to take care of us after the funeral. Many of these people were themselves poor. We would soon be left to fend for ourselves.

CHAPTER 12

The following morning we heard a commotion and everyone's eyes turned toward the gate.

A spectacle of men, women, and cattle approached our compound. The men were dressed as tribesmen poised for a battle. They wore cowhides over their clothes and some had vines wrapped around their heads. Others wore huge feathered hats. Their faces were painted in white and red, like traditional Luo warriors. They carried spears pointed straight ahead, as though they were ready to throw them.

One or two men beat small drums that produced somber, eerie sounds. Another played a long bull's horn in rhythm with the drum. The warrior-like tribesmen hopped and jumped in rhythm—first on one leg and then the other—as they slowly made their way into the compound.

"There, there it is. Kill it!" one of the men yelled, and they all began shouting. Baby jumped and held onto my leg.

"Those warriors have come to give Baba a send-off to the next world," I told her. "They are here to destroy Death so it can haunt our people no more."

"Can they actually do that?" Baby asked.

"Let's watch and see," I replied. I had vowed to treat Baby less like a toddler and more like the schoolgirl she now was.

"There! There!" The warriors grunted and charged like bulls, chasing Death one way, then sharply turning to catch it in another direction. Every now and then one of them would stop, lift his spear above his shoulder, aim at the ground, and strike at something unseen. But I knew Death wasn't there, in the ground. It was in Baba. And in Abeth's parents. By now, Death was lurking inside so many of the bodies around Koromo, maybe even in those that circled our family compound. Each thrust of the spear was supposed to signify that Death had just been killed. I wished I could take comfort from the ritual. But these days, it didn't seem as if a spear would be powerful enough to destroy this slow and greedy plague preying on my village.

The women who had arrived with the warriors were running around the compound, in and out of the house, screaming and yelling in high-pitched voices. They were enacting the sadness that Death caused. I let my eyelids close for a minute, thinking I might rest my tired eyes.

"Auma! Auma! Aiiiii!" Baby's screaming jolted my eyelids open. I should have known better than to take my eyes off the spectacle. I knew how unpredictable a yard full of cows could be, running amok in places you wouldn't imagine. One of them was charging straight at us, and didn't give any sign that it was going to slow down.

I scooped Baby up with one arm and dove to the right. The heifer missed us by inches, and headed straight into the house, handler in tow, through the sitting room and out the back door.

The uproar of laughter in the middle of Baba's funeral was uncanny. As I watched Baby and my brothers throw their heads back, laughing from deep in their bellies, I couldn't help but think this was Baba's doing. When he was well, he had always found things funny, even when Mama was angry. Maybe Baba had figured out a way, at least for the moment, to kill Death himself. I smiled at the thought.

♦♦♦

The burial service was quick, and people began to leave during the late afternoon. That night, I lay down to sleep early, hoping I could doze off despite their chatter.

I covered my head with a blanket, so everyone would assume I was sleeping and not ask me to run an errand. That was all I had done the whole week.

Within minutes the people nearby started whispering to each other.

"His symptoms were that of a person who had been cursed with . . . you know . . . ," someone said. "Anyone who dies of . . . you know . . . has not acted according to tradition. The bad spirits have had their revenge."

My blood ran cold. These people were saying that my father had died because he'd broken our traditions. If he'd seen the medicine man, would he be alive? Was our God wrong? Were the ancient Luo beliefs right?

I thought about all the times I'd asked Mama questions and she'd given me simple answers. Maybe that was better, not knowing. Or maybe the worst feeling came from only knowing half of something, and never being able to get a complete answer.

And maybe the adults weren't hiding things from me. Maybe they really didn't know.

That thought scared me more than the idea that Baba might have had . . . AIDS. That he could have lived if we'd only gone to the medicine man. That God didn't exist. Or that He did, and He'd taken Baba from us on purpose.

I figured I could probably handle whatever answers were out there, at least in time. But what I couldn't fathom was that all the adults around me were as blind as children, throwing spears at invisible things, choosing to make the truth whatever they wanted it to be.

It took me a long time to meet sleep that night, but I finally gave in to my exhaustion when I realized the answers I sought certainly were not inside my own head.

CHAPTER 13

After Baba's burial, we were left with only one cow. Just as I'd feared, all the rest of our cattle, along with all our chickens and goats, had been slaughtered for food to feed the crowds of people who came to honor Baba and console us. For the first few weeks, neighbors occasionally brought food to share when they dropped by to check on us. But soon our food supply dwindled to almost nothing.

And then there was school to worry about. We missed three weeks of classes, and by early February I was eager to get back and catch up before the end of the term. It felt good to be running with the track team again, and it felt even better to see Abeth regularly. Now we both were *kiye*, orphans. Even though Mama was still alive, a child with only one parent was still considered a *kich*.

I quickly got used to the casual taunts of my classmates. Orphans were easy targets for bullying. The female teachers strictly punished any student who called us names, but the male teachers often pretended not to hear. The boys especially seemed to enjoy teasing us.

Except for Abuya. After he chased me, the principal had sentenced him to dig out a tree stump as his punishment. Since then, he hadn't said a word to me. I'd heard Peter say he was embarrassed for chasing me and causing my fall, that he thought I hated him.

But I had far bigger problems than Abuya now.

How would we afford next year's school dues? Kiye were expected to pay in full and on time, just like those who had parents. Anyone who couldn't pay was not allowed to come back.

I decided to ask God for help. I figured it couldn't hurt. I prayed that we would never miss a payment of our tuition. I also prayed for something that would help me understand this mysterious deadly plague, this scourge that may have killed my father, this thing called AIDS. I still had a hard time saying the word, even inside my head.

◆◆◆

Mr. Osogo, the science teacher, stood at the front of the classroom. "Today we are going to discuss diseases in your body, specifically those that can be spread from person to person—sexually transmitted diseases."

On the board he wrote *STDs*.

I sat up straighter in my seat. This was like an answer to my prayer.

The boys began to squirm and I heard a low giggle. A few of the girls looked down, their faces flushed with embarrassment. No adult had ever talked to us about sex. The topic was only rarely discussed between friends, and never around the opposite sex. Maybe in Class Eight we were grown up enough to hear about such things . . .

I whipped out my notebook, pushing aside my embarrassment.

"Who can tell me the name of an STD?" Mr. Osogo asked.

"Syphilis!" shouted Mika.

"Gonorrhea!" other voices chorused from the back of the room.

"Good contributions. We talked about these diseases last week." Clearly I'd missed a lot while I was out of school. "Today we're going to focus on—"

"Teacher!" cut in the class clown, Peter. He didn't wait for Mr. Osogo to call on him before asking his question. "Nobody has had sex in this class, so why do we need to learn about these diseases?"

"Look at Peter pretending to be innocent," someone in the back mumbled.

Everyone roared with nervous laughter. "Anyone who acts like a child should be prepared for a spanking," said Mr. Osogo sternly, and order was quickly restored.

"But to answer your question, Peter," Mr. Osogo went on with a very serious look. "We are trying to prepare you for the future. According to statistics, 30 percent of you will not live to the age of thirty-five. That's three out of ten of you. There are forty-five students in this room, so that means about thirteen."

He walked through the rows, tapping on every third child and motioning for them to stand up. "Everyone standing could be dead. These are the odds."

Absolute silence swept through the class.

"Can anyone tell me the symptoms of any one venereal disease?" he asked. He wrote *syphilis* and *gonorrhea* on the blackboard with a broken piece of chalk no longer than a paper clip.

Again Peter yelled his response. "Teacher, I know about gonorrhea! That thing is *painful*."

"How do you know?" Tito jumped in.

"My brother had a friend who was sick. He said that the man had unbearable pain in his privates, and couldn't walk. That's all I know," said Peter. He was no longer acting goofy. He wore a pained expression.

Mr. Osogo said he was right.

As I listened to my classmates, who obviously knew more people who'd had sex than I knew, I was disgusted. They said you'd get sores on your privates, nasty itches, and fevers. I wondered how anyone with a brain in their head could have sex after they'd learned about such horrible diseases. I nervously glanced at Abeth, who, like me, looked very uncomfortable. I wanted to catch Abuya's eye to see his reaction, but I was too embarrassed.

I turned my head back to the front of the class. As unsettling as this lesson was, I wanted so badly to know the truth.

Slowly, Mr. Osogo wrote new letters on the board: *HIV/AIDS*.

"Auma, can you explain this acronym?"

I gave him a blank look.

"Auma, I'm talking to you. Help us out here."

"I don't know, sir," I replied.

"You should have read about this in last night's homework, Auma. If you had done your homework, you would know the answer," Mr. Osogo said sternly, as he looked to call on somebody else. It didn't matter that today was my first day back at school since Baba died, that I was a partial orphan now. No excuses allowed.

"Human immunodeficiency virus," Tabu said firmly and confidently. Mr. Osogo wrote the words on the blackboard.

"How about AIDS?" he continued, turning slowly and scanning the classroom. "Abeth, can you help us?"

"Yes sir. It means acquired immunodeficiency syndrome."

Silence fell over the whole class. I hoped Mr. Osogo was going to tell us everything—what this disease was, whether it was the cause of all the deaths, whether it could be cured.

"Like all viruses, HIV has many street names. You and your friends might call it Slim. Or, if you're braver than the average fearful citizen of Koromo, you call it *Ukimwi*—AIDS." He had the attention of everyone in the class. Forty-five teenagers stared straight ahead, soaking in every word.

"When you are healthy, your body's immune system fights off infections and illnesses. We discussed that in Chapter Two last week. When your body becomes infected with HIV, the virus attacks the immune system, leaving your body vulnerable to everything. The virus creeps inside your cells and reproduces. Once you have it, you have it for the rest of your life, at least where modern medicine stands. No one, not even the wazungu in Europe or America, has found a cure. And most people show no symptoms for months, even years."

I wanted to ask how someone could get HIV—if all the rumors I'd heard were right, that you had to "walk around." I raised my hand straight up in the air without waiting for question time. I did not even wait for him give me permission to speak. I just blurted out the question.

"Mr. Osogo, sir, how do people contract HIV?"

I could feel the heat on my face as I waited for his answer. The few seconds of silence were like an eternity. My heart was pounding and my palms sweating. But it was done, I had asked the big question.

After what seemed like a long pause, Mr. Osogo

said, "Thank you for that excellent question, Auma—though I would've preferred for you to wait until question time." Addressing the whole class, he said, "You may have heard rumors about how it's spread. That you can only get it if you're a sinner. Wrong."

I gulped.

"Yes, it is true that you get it through having sex with someone who is infected. Keep in mind, that means if you're married and your spouse contracts the disease, you could get it just by sleeping with your spouse. But there are also other ways—sharing needles, wiping someone's bloody wound without wearing gloves, or letting a bodily fluid pass into your body through broken skin or membrane."

A few gasps echoed from the back of the room.

"As far as research stands," he went on, "I have to let you know that it does not appear you can contract HIV through kissing. Saliva is safe."

Several of my classmates breathed audible sighs of relief. Although I'd never kissed anyone, I was sure a few of the girls in the class had secretly kissed boys before.

"But even if you're still a virgin you have cause to worry."

The same boys and girls who had just relaxed were tense once again.

"You can contract it through any kind of wound or cut in your mouth, if you make contact with the bodily fluids of someone who is infected. And once you've got it, you're not safe either. Every time you are exposed to the virus again, it increases its killing power."

Mr. Osogo said lots of people died because of opportunistic diseases like tuberculosis, and that not everyone showed all the symptoms at the same time. Then he described some of the most common symptoms: weight loss, fatigue, a cough . .

They were identical to Baba's.

At this point I felt like I was going to die. I had my answer.

Could my father really have died from AIDS? He wasn't a drug user, so he wouldn't have shared needles with anyone. He hadn't mentioned that he was taking care of anyone who was sick, although I knew him to be kindhearted enough to do so. And he'd been married to only one woman and she wasn't infected. I paused in my thoughts. Mama *was* the only woman, wasn't she?

I didn't want to consider the possibility.

And what about Abeth's parents? These symptoms were similar to what I saw happen to them. But how did they contract the disease? Maybe at the hospital when Abeth's mother was giving birth to Supa. The nurse may have used a dirty needle to give her pain medication . . .

The questions stampeded through me. Why weren't there a hundred Mr. Osogos dragging blackboards into the middle of the market and explaining this to everyone? Why was even the disease's name hidden beneath a layer of *you knows* and stupid nicknames?

I knew it was going to be up to us, those who fell somewhere between childhood and maturity, to do something.

How were we to educate our parents, who thrived on rumor, without a science textbook and a teacher to steer their brains in the right direction?

Mr. Osogo continued, explaining that there was not yet a cure for AIDS and that the only way to avoid it was to keep from having sex with a person who was already infected. Then he added that if we knew anyone with the disease, we should wear gloves when helping them go to the bathroom or cleaning their wounds. He also said that since many of us girls were probably only a few years away from marriage, it was important that people get tested before they would be fit for marriage.

Mama had always said she didn't want me to get pregnant before I got married, but she must have known about these diseases, too. And had she known that even a married woman could be in danger, if her husband had the disease?

I swallowed hard. If Baba . . .

I pushed that thought out of my mind and replaced it with a less frightening one: I *will not get married*. As long as I could keep that resolution, I felt fairly sure that I would be safe from AIDS.

But what about Mama?

CHAPTER 14

After school I wanted more time to think, to clear my head, so I headed toward the place where Haha flowed so beautifully during the rainy season. But like everything else in my life, Haha was dried up.

Deep in my thoughts, I knelt by the soko and scooped water into the mangled pail I had brought. Juma had accidentally broken our only plastic bucket, so Musa and I had collected pieces of broken plastic from wherever we could, then burned and melted them to seal them together.

"How are you, Auma?" a voice from behind me said gently. I nearly fell into the soko with shock.

I turned my head sharply to see a tall man sitting on a large rock. When I recognized him as my neighbor Otito, I relaxed a bit. "Fine, thank you."

Otito was a widower. He'd remained shut in since his wife died, and his children were older and often out of the house. I felt sorry for him—a grown man having to bear the chore of fetching water, a duty usually reserved for women and children. When I realized I was staring at how thin he had become, I lowered my eyes.

"I'm glad I ran into you here, Auma. I've been meaning to talk to you," Otito said.

"Oh?" I hurried to fill my pail. Of all my neighbors, Otito was the one I knew the least.

"Yes, Auma, you can help me."

"Oh, I'm sorry, sir. Yes, of course I can fill your pail for you." I looked up and noticed he had no pail with him.

The hairs on the back of my neck stood up. How long had he been watching me?

When Otito stood, I lifted the pail onto my head, even though it wasn't completely full yet. "I have to be getting home, Mama is expecting me soon," I lied.

I started to walk past him. He stepped in front of me and blocked my path.

"Excuse me, I need to pass," I said.

"But I'm not finished talking to you."

Dark memories flashed through my mind: the

day in the woods with my brothers, Abuya chasing me. I didn't understand men. I did nothing to ask for their attention, made every effort to avoid enticing them . . .

Sweat ran down my back. I didn't want to disrespect Otito, my elder, but I knew what he wanted.

"I don't know you," I said, trying to brush past him, hoping he would leave it at that.

"You will know me," he leered.

Then he lunged at me.

With all the force I could muster, I dumped the water over his head, smashing his head with the pail. Then I grabbed the pail and ran.

It felt good to run. I pretended I was little again, Mama holding a piece of nguru at the finish line and I keeping my eye on the goal as I ran. I imagined the clouds on the horizon were those light brown blocks of sugarcane juice, and I didn't dare take my eyes off them until I reached home.

Except when I reached home, there was no sweet jaggery to taste. At home, there were only the reminders of how life had become so desperate for everyone in Koromo, including our family.

"Auma! What's the matter?" cried Mama when she saw me. "Sit, child. Calm down."

Breathlessly, I tried to tell Mama what had just happened to me, hoping she wouldn't be ashamed of me for disrespecting an elder. At first Mama was speechless. Then, once she'd heard the whole story, she looked furious. "Auma," she said through clenched teeth, "I don't want you to go to the stream by yourself again. Ever."

I nodded meekly.

Then her shoulders slumped and she let out a long, wavering breath. "You're lucky Baba was your father. You got good legs and a good brain from him."

I realized then that she wasn't angry at me, but at Otito for what he'd tried to do.

"Come inside now, Auma. There's much that needs telling."

I wondered if Mama was finally going to uncover all the secrets that only she and the walls knew. So far, I'd gotten more answers in one day than I had in all the years since Death began haunting Koromo. My stomach cramped. The more answers I found, the worse life seemed to get.

"Auma, I know that you've started going to the moon." This wasn't what I'd expected her to talk about. "It doesn't matter that you didn't tell me. I assume you didn't want to worry me."

She looked away and then down, clearly hurt. I wanted to tell her that I hadn't kept my periods a secret because I didn't trust *her*. I'd been worried about how Dani would react—worried that she'd push even harder for me to get married. Even if Mama opposed it, Dani had a way of trying to control our lives.

I swallowed. "Sorry, Mama. I didn't want you to keep me home from school like the other girls. I stole one of Baby's old blankets to make strips. I'm sorry."

Mama hushed me gently. She walked slowly to the chair and sat down, looking out the window to make sure my younger siblings were occupied.

"Auma, you're growing up. You'll have to get used to other people seeing you as a woman. Especially men."

"I know I have to be careful, Mama. You taught me that."

She looked down once more. "It's hard for me to give you advice about men. In truth, the older I get the less I feel I understand them." I wondered if she was talking about Baba. "It's rumored that Otito has the new disease. I suspect that he wanted you to help him cure it."

"Me?" I was puzzled.

"Many of the older men in the village say that if a man sleeps with a virgin, he will be cured of the disease."

"But that sounds ridiculous, Mama!"

She didn't answer.

"Mama, it's not true, is it? Mr. Osogo told us something entirely different just today in science class . . ."

"Shhh." Mama put her finger to my lips. "I don't know about science class, but I do suspect this rumor is false. And I fear that many desperate men will be making young girls sick."

Her voice now became stronger.

"Today, you ran for a good reason. A very good reason."

Mama rubbed her temples and lay back on the chair, which was unusual, but it had been a long day. She looked exhausted, and perhaps it was my fault. I felt tired, too, but there was dinner to be made and a few chores left to finish. If I let Mama rest, I knew she'd have more strength tomorrow. We'd talk more then. There would be an entire lifetime to ask Mama everything I wanted to know.

While she rested, I went outside where Musa,

Juma, and Baby were playing. Dani was watching them. They looked so innocent, running in a circle and laughing. I wanted to run in that circle, too, and stop the sun high in the sky. But the chores were waiting for me. I was a woman now.

◆◆◆

A few days later I was on my way to the shopping center to buy more over-the-counter pain medication for my mother. As I rounded a bend in the road, I saw Abuya coming my direction. My heart sank. I decided to take a detour around a small bush.

Abuya was not going to have that. "Hey, why are you trying to hide from me?" he called out.

"I'm not," I responded.

"The path is right here. Look, Auma, I'm not going to hurt you. I just want to talk to you."

My heart beat out of rhythm.

"You know I never meant to keep chasing you like that. I only kept going because I thought it was a joke." He moved toward the bush.

I slowly walked out from behind the bush. I cleared my throat. "But why did you even block the doorway in the first place?"

He ducked his head. "I'm sorry. I should have backed off. At least forgive me, even if you don't want to be friends with me."

For a moment I wondered what it would be like to be friends with Abuya. Was it even possible? After all, he'd made it clear he wanted more than friendship . . .

In a rush he added, "But why do you always try to avoid us boys? You don't talk to us like some of the other girls do."

"I'm not other girls and I have nothing to talk about."

"Is that why you ran away?"

"No," I said impatiently. "You want a reason? I'm far too busy doing my schoolwork and running errands for my mother."

"You can at least talk while we're at school. You don't have to be so hostile," he said quietly.

I knew it was true that I was hostile. But that seemed to be the only way to keep boys from getting too close. If I'd learned anything over the past few months, it was that avoiding boys outright was the safest course of action.

"Well, I'll see about that," I said—mostly because I wanted this conversation to end. I tried to smile.

"I have to go now. See you at school." I started walking slowly away.

"Okay, thanks, I'll see you at school tomorrow," he called.

I breathed a sigh of relief. I was glad I hadn't run from this situation. Abuya was a kind boy, and it wasn't his fault that my world didn't make sense anymore. Still, I felt more convinced than ever that a real friendship was unrealistic. I could wish him well, but I had to look out for myself.

CHAPTER 15

I felt hopeful now that I would be able to complete Class Eight. If only I could grow slowly so that Mama wouldn't have to buy another uniform. Already, I had outgrown the only one I had. I'd be kicked out of school if any of the teachers noticed how short it was.

Once again, Mama found a way to make something from nothing. During the term break in April, she had the village tailor add a strip of fabric to the bottom of my skirt, making the dress longer.

It looked hideous.

On the first day of the new term in May, I felt embarrassed putting on my school uniform. *Maybe this will at least keep the boys away*, I thought, trying to console myself. I pulled on my ragged jumper, squeezing it down past my full bust. I felt like it was going to pop open under my arm if I moved too much.

Once I was dressed, I searched the kitchen for any leftovers from breakfast, but the cupboard was empty, and the only food I could find was a few minuscule drips of porridge that Baby had spilled on the table. An army of ants fought for the remains. It seemed like even the ants at our house were starving. I closed my eyes and wished I could climb on a pile of food ten times my size.

My siblings and I left for school without one piece of sweet potato or helping of porridge. We'd have to get used to going without breakfast and lunch. I figured running would keep my mind off my empty stomach. "Beat you there!" I yelled to the others as I took off down the road.

I crossed into the schoolyard just ahead of Juma. "Nice run," he said in between breaths as Musa whizzed past us.

"Yes, it was," I replied honestly. But now I felt weak and dizzy.

Juma helped me straighten back up. "Take it easy. You're probably low on energy because we didn't have breakfast," he said matter-of-factly. Satisfied that I was all right, he headed off to class.

My rush of good feeling disappeared. What would I do if I couldn't run well anymore?

"Nice skirt, kich," my classmate Peter laughed as he passed by.

My cheeks went cold again, then hot with anger, before I was able to cool them down with a few slow, deep breaths. So much for boys not noticing me.

Abeth appeared at my side. "Sometimes I wish the boys were more creative with their insults, don't you?" she said wryly.

I knew she was trying to cheer me up, but Peter's words still stung. "Abeth, is this what you've been going through all this time? It's as if there's no right choice for me to make. If I walk around with a uniform that's too short, I get expelled. If I make my uniform longer, I get ridiculed."

She shrugged. "Ignore that idiot. He's just jealous that you're taller than him." She struck a pose. "I hear that tall and skinny is a good thing in the city. People think girls who look like there's no food at home are attractive!"

We burst out laughing at the idea that men would actually like girls who were flat as sticks. Joking eased the pain of being orphans and our silent fear of the future.

"So if we lived there we'd be in style," I sighed. "But who cares if you're beautiful when you're hungry?" I rubbed my stomach. "I'd rather be ugly and satisfied." We both laughed again as we headed for our classroom.

But suddenly I thought of how poor Supa had wasted away. A few months ago Abeth never would've made a joke about starving. I was amazed at how she'd managed to pick up the pieces of her life and carry on, refusing to let her sorrow hold her back.

◆◆◆

During all my classes, my imagination was full of "food rescues." I daydreamed about light brown, sweet nguru falling from the sky, and sticking my tongue out to catch it. I imagined ripe sugar apples bigger than my head. I mentally cracked each one open and sucked out the white, meaty flesh, as the white juice dripped down and stained my dress. But the end-of-day bell zapped me out of my trance. I half-ran, half-walked home—afraid to overtire myself but motivated by the prospect of an evening meal. At least supper was one meal we could still count on.

Mama wasn't home, and she hadn't finished weeding the newly extended vegetable garden.

I picked up the hoe before Dani could tell me it needed to be done. I motioned to Juma to get the other hoe and help me out. He dropped his book bag and went to get it. Musa was already taking care of the animals. Even Baby was working, sweeping the veranda. For the moment, I felt as though our yard knew no children anymore.

"What does that man want here?" Juma muttered under his breath.

I'd been so focused on weeding that I hadn't noticed the visitor arrive. It was Akuku, our neighbor, now sitting under the guava tree talking to Dani.

Akuku was one of the neighbors who rarely came around when Baba was alive. I didn't recall him attending the burial or bringing any gifts. Yet he'd shown up three times in the past week to talk to Dani or Mama. I didn't like him much. He seemed rather old, idle-minded, and shady. The veins in his neck and forehead popped out like branches and his eyes were always twittering back and forth under half-closed lids, as if he were spying on the entire village.

I shifted my position so I could keep a steady eye on Akuku.

After a few minutes he got up to leave—and nearly ran into Mama as she came through the gate. The bucket atop her head teetered, but she steadied it with great effort, and only a dash of water spilled over the rim.

I couldn't hear what Akuku said to my mother. But after he left, I watched Mama walk into the hut and noticed that her feet didn't hit the ground hard anymore. Since I was a baby, whenever Mama was approaching I knew. I could always hear her purposeful footsteps. She had a confident walk that suggested great strength. But now, if I hadn't been watching her, she'd have sneaked in without my noticing, just like Akuku.

I finished weeding the garden and helped Mama make sukuma wiki without any tomatoes or onions. That night, I choked down the bland greens with the doughy ugali. I could feel my stomach filling quickly, though, so I didn't complain.

After supper, I swept the kitchen's dirt floor as usual so it would be clear for Juma and Musa to sleep on. Then Baby and I went to the sitting room and lay down on our mat. It was always easier to fall asleep when there was something in my stomach.

"Did you hear that?"

I woke up to Baby tugging at my T-shirt collar. I listened. A shuffling noise came from outside the window.

"It's probably just the cow scratching herself," I said, trying to calm Baby. "Or a bat." Sometimes bats hit the wall or roof as they swooped for insects. I gently patted Baby's back. "Let's go back to sleep."

Baby believed me, tucked herself under the sheet again, and closed her eyes.

The shuffling noise grew louder, closer.

"Who's there?" I called, mimicking the way I always heard Dani call out.

No response.

Just the cow or a bat, I repeated in my head. It was ridiculous to think it could be something else . . . like a night runner.

I rolled over and scolded myself for how childish I was being. Baby had fallen back to sleep almost instantly. But I tossed back and forth on the mat, unable to settle myself.

Now I heard light footsteps outside the window. I strained to hear better, not daring to breathe. Yes, the footsteps were coming closer. My heart started thumping.

The footsteps passed the window, before growing faint again. Whoever it was walked very fast. And they were leaving. They'd been here the whole time.

I wondered again if a night runner was out there, here to scare us because Baba was no longer around. But no one hopped out and said "Boo!" The footsteps had gone quickly past the window and around the side of the house.

Thoughts about night runners raced through my mind until I fell asleep. I decided not to tell Mama about what I'd heard. I couldn't bear to add another worry line to her face. She seemed to have so many already. But I kept wondering about those soft footsteps outside, those feet creeping through the night.

CHAPTER 16

A week later, I held a burning log in my hand and crouched behind the kitchen, waiting for our mysterious visitor to show himself. For several nights in a row, I'd heard his footsteps, always around the same time each night. Often he woke Baby, and then I had to lie to her—say that she'd just dreamed the noise or that it was just an animal—to get her back to sleep. I was tired of lying. Tired of lying awake in the dark wondering what was going on.

Tonight I would put a stop to it. This night runner, or whoever he was, would learn to stop lurking around our compound.

There he was, coming through the gate and crossing the compound. Just as he passed between the main house and the kitchen, I jumped out into the open and whacked the intruder on the arm with my weapon.

He let out a howl and staggered backward. In the light of the log's flames, I made out his face.

Akuku.

In my surprise, I dropped the log, and it lay smoldering on the ground as Mama raced out of the house. "What is this? What's going on?"

"Your crazy daughter attacked me!" roared Akuku. "What's wrong with this child? See what she's done to my arm?"

"I'm so sorry," Mama said to him. "I'll speak to her. It's probably best if you go now."

Akuku stormed out of the compound while I stared at Mama in shock. Why had she apologized to Akuku when I'd just caught him sneaking around our compound in the middle of the night? "Mama—"

"Auma, go back to bed," Mama said sharply.

"I was just trying to—"

"Make sure that log is doused and go back to bed." She turned and went back inside before I could say more.

◆◆◆

"I nearly killed the man. He got a burn on his arm," I told Abeth as we warmed up before track practice.

"You mean the night runner?" Abeth asked.

"Yes. Only he's not a night runner. It was Akuku! He's the one who's been coming to our home all these nights." I bent down to stretch my legs.

Abeth gasped. "Oh no! Your mother is being inherited, Auma! This man must be your mother's new 'husband.'"

"What?" I shot back up, staring in disbelief. "Husband? I didn't think remarriage would be such a sneaky business." I couldn't picture Mama, once a sturdy and proud woman who laughed, getting involved with such an unattractive, ill-humored man. He was nothing like Baba. He had never even tried to have a conversation with us children. There was no way Mama could love him.

"No, not an *actual* husband," said Abeth. "Just someone who represents the family when a male figure is needed. Men like Akuku are willing to fulfill those traditional requirements in exchange for—you know."

I couldn't believe Mama would do something like that without my knowledge. And with Akuku, of all people! Over and over again, she'd warned me to stay away from boys—to not let any man take advantage of me. I was sure she would never willingly agree to this kind of arrangement.

Abeth's voice dropped to a whisper. "Auma, I've heard the women say that Akuku has already inherited many women whose husbands have died of the modern disease."

I swallowed hard. The idea of a woman being sold to a man made my empty stomach churn. How could it be that adults hadn't figured out that some traditions had to go? People in Koromo were still doing what they'd always done, only with a dangerous twist.

I hoped that somebody out there was *not* following these traditions. Surely I couldn't be the only one opposed to this practice. Some other women must be against it too.

But were they able to say no? It certainly seemed as if Mama didn't have a choice right now.

Pastor Joseph would definitely disapprove of such a practice. It obviously went against Christian teachings. *I'm on the right path*, I thought. But even the church could only change so much about our lives here.

I had heard enough talk about "this is our culture and there is nothing you can do." Maybe in the city, things were different.

"Auma," Abeth said quietly. "Most of the women Akuku has inherited are dead."

Mr. Ouma's voice boomed. "On your marks, ladies!"

How on earth could I concentrate on running now? I tried picturing Mama standing at the finish line, with a piece of nguru. That always motivated me to run fast when I was a small girl. But I was a woman now.

Instead of imagining my mother's smiling face, I saw her as pale—the color of light brown nguru, like a ghost. I saw Akuku holding her so tightly that she might suffocate. Lying on the ground next to her were piles of women's bodies. Akuku's corpses.

I had my target. I took my mark.

"Get set," Mr. Ouma called, holding up a piece of red cloth. "Go!" He whipped the red flag down to his side.

My legs burst forward, dashing to save Mama from Akuku. I sped ahead, my heels kicking up fresh dirt. As I got closer I checked to my sides to see if anyone was close. I was leading by a good margin. I turned to see Mama's image, but she was gone. My left toes caught the back of my ankle and I plummeted, face first, to the dirt. By the time I lifted my chest from the ground, nearly everyone in Class Eight had passed me. I had taken my eyes off the finish line. In that split second, all was lost.

"She fell!" a few voices in the crowd shouted, followed by faint laughter.

Now, my insides felt as worthless as the shouts of failure coming from every direction. Then an unidentified voice yelled out the word I hated most: "Kich!" Orphan.

"Shut up!" Abeth called out immediately, coming to my defense. She made fists with both her hands. Everyone hushed.

She put out a hand and helped me up. I could see two angry teachers searching for the culprit who'd yelled the insult, but no one came forward.

"Name-calling will not be tolerated," one of the teachers loudly declared. I looked at the teacher's waving finger and hand on her hip, then shifted my gaze to Abeth's protective scowl. Who cared if I was an orphan? I had someone watching out for me.

"Again," I said, and stomped back to the starting line. No one followed. I didn't care if I was going to run alone. I was going to finish, and in my fastest time ever. I wouldn't give up, like Mama had. I wasn't going to settle for less than I deserved, like Mama. And I wasn't going to let my only chance of going to secondary school on a track scholarship be taken away because of one silly fall. Since the day I was born, I'd beaten the odds. This time would be no different.

I took my mark and waited for the signal.

CHAPTER 17

I arrived home from school still sprinting victoriously. Before I even reached the gate, I started calling out my story to Mama. Inside the compound, I found her lying limp in the sun.

"Mama, what's the matter? Are you sick?" I asked, suddenly anxious.

"I don't feel well," she said, her voice soft and shaky.

"Is it malaria?"

"No. Go get a blanket and cover me. I'm cold."

This sounded crazy. The sun was hot. And what did she mean, *no*? It was like she knew what she had, but she hadn't seen a doctor in months.

I went inside, got a blanket, and came out onto the veranda. I covered her and stood silently for a moment.

"Mama, why don't I take you to the doctor?" I blurted out nervously.

"Auma, look at us. We don't even have food to eat. What would I pay the doctor with?" she said, looking away.

My mother really was giving up. This was the woman who could make anything out of nothing and now, for the first time, I heard despair in her voice. Ever since Baba had died, we had been suffering, but not until now had Mama sounded like this.

"But Mama," I insisted, "you can go to the government hospital in Homa Bay. Treatment there will be cheaper—maybe even free."

Mama looked at me with tears in her eyes. I tried to look at her the way she used to look at me, encouragingly.

"I'll try," she whispered. A tear tumbled down her cheek. "I'll borrow some money for the bus fare."

Even more tears coursed down her face. I tried my best to console her, but I wasn't good at it. It had always been the other way around. Children weren't supposed to comfort adults. All of Koromo seemed upside-down, and it seemed like it was intent on staying that way.

◆◆◆

Mama managed to borrow some money to see the Homa Bay physician. I wondered if it came from Akuku, but I learned from Dani that it came from Mama Benta.

After school, I waited nervously for her to return. I swept the veranda about five times, singing under my breath. If I wasn't running, singing kept my mind busy and gave me the motivation to keep going.

At last Mama came home with a bag of medications and an informational pamphlet. I skimmed over the pamphlet, which just explained that she was supposed to take these medications every day and that she needed to maintain a nutritious diet. Nothing about her actual diagnosis.

"What did the doctor say is wrong?" I asked.

"Well, my body isn't absorbing enough food. So I'm losing energy and becoming feverish." Mama seemed annoyed—not at me but at her uncooperative body. "The medications will help me feel better, don't worry."

She was clearly exhausted, so I helped her into bed. "Auma, thank you. I'm glad you insisted I go."

She closed her eyes to tell me the conversation was over. Although I felt some relief, Mama still wasn't herself.

◆◆◆

Weeks passed. Mama would feel fine for a while, and then she'd get ill again. She could no longer sell ropes or work for the lady who sold pots in the market. I thought we were going to have to start begging. Food had been scarce for a long time, and now that the rains were gone for the season, the garden looked pathetic. I'd missed a great deal of school and trial races during the first term—January to March. I hoped Mama would get better before the start of the second term—May to July—when the real track meets began.

I stared at the sky, wondering where all the rain had gone. Then I stared at our sad garden. My siblings mimicked me, turning their heads from the sky to the garden, and I knew my siblings were just as afraid as I.

"Auma, what are we going to do?" Juma asked me. "If Mama doesn't get better fast enough, we will have nothing to eat."

I had no answer for him.

"I need to find work over the break," he declared firmly. "And I can continue it on the weekends after the break if Mama's still sick." He drew himself up like a little man, and my heart filled with pain for him. He was so young—barely eleven—yet he reminded me so much of Baba.

I wanted to tell him I could take care of everything, that I could get a job and clean and cook. But I knew I had to devote some of the break time to catching up on all the schoolwork I'd missed, in addition to all my regular chores. My perfect As had slumped to a B-minus average during the first term. If I wanted to pass my exams at the end of the year and earn a scholarship to secondary school, I had to study.

"I think that's a good idea," I encouraged Juma, though I was filled with guilt. "Let's ask Mama Benta if she has something for you to do."

I knew the Bimas had money to spare. Mama Benta and her husband each wore a different outfit every day of the week. They'd brought many gifts to Baba's funeral. Still, the rumors of how they treated village workers loomed in my mind. I hoped the gossip was wrong—because I couldn't think of anyone else in Koromo who could afford to hire my brother.

"I'll work too," Musa chimed in.

"Good. We'll go see Mama Benta right now, then. Let me do the talking." I grabbed Baby's hand and we left the pitiful garden behind.

All of us walked up to the Bima family's home. The front gate wasn't rusted like ours. And the house was more than four times the size of ours, built of solid concrete—not mud bricks or wood. The burgundy-colored paint didn't have a single chip in it.

Mama Benta herself came to the front door to answer my knock.

I blurted out, "My mother is asking if you have anything for Juma and Musa to do for pay."

"Oh, come on in, Auma," Mama Benta said. She opened the door wider and led us inside. She gestured, inviting us to sit down on a white sofa with a flower pattern. We all sat, and Baby bounced happily next to me. It was only my second or third time sitting on a real sofa, and probably Baby's first. I put my hand on her knee gently, to stop her from bouncing.

"Is your mother not okay?" Mama Benta inquired.

"Well, she hasn't been feeling well lately, and it's

slowing down her market business." Not a lie—just not the whole truth.

"Oh, I'm so sorry to hear that," Mama Benta said, and she sounded sincere. "We can definitely find something for your brothers to do. Let me send you word tomorrow."

"Thank you," I said, and the others echoed me, even Baby.

Mama Benta stood up, and I gestured to my siblings to get up, too. "Now make sure you tell your mother that I will visit her." As she led me back to the door, she gently took my shoulders. "Auma, you're welcome to let us know whenever you need help."

I thanked her again. Her good-bye was a reassuring smile. *The Bimas are good people,* I decided, *no matter what other people say.*

I couldn't wait to get home. At last, I felt a new energy—to cook, to continue doing the chores. I began to run as fast as I could, leaving my siblings to catch up. If Juma or Musa went right to work, we would be able to buy more food, and maybe even soap! Oh, how I missed the sweet smell of soap!

When my siblings caught up to me at the gate, I put my arm out to stop them. "Listen. No one tells Mama about Mama Benta, or about you boys working."

"Why can't we tell Mama?" Baby whined.

I squatted down so that my eyes were level with Baby's. "Because she probably wouldn't allow it if she found out. You know how she doesn't want us to beg or take handouts. But if the boys don't go to work, we'll have no money and no food, and Mama will probably get sicker."

That was probably true. The number one thing the hospital pamphlet had said was to feed her well, with good, nutritious foods. Right now we couldn't even do that.

"While Mama is sick, I'm in charge. And I say you can't tell Mama where we went today. It's a secret. Do you understand, Baby?"

"All right," Baby whimpered, on the verge of tears. *I guess this is what it means to be the eldest,* I told myself. *You take charge.* In the past, when Mama felt I was being lazy, that's what she'd always said—take charge. So I was doing as she'd asked.

I just hadn't realized how hard it would be. It sounded so glorious, the idea of making all the decisions. Doing whatever you wanted. None of this seemed like what I wanted, though.

Turning to my brothers, I said, "While we're home, we must work together without fighting. Mama needs to hear nothing but good children. That will encourage her. Go and finish your chores now!"

We entered the yard together but quickly scattered. In the kitchen, I began making a fire for cooking. As I pulled a stick loose from the firewood heap, I realized I'd never been in charge quite like this. I had to hold on to the belief that Mama would be okay soon—that we could all go back to the way we used to be. But deep inside me, I wasn't so sure. I thought about the possibilities—about Mama, about Akuku—and I felt a chill run through my body.

I heard one of my brothers coming over to help; I quickly bent down to break the firewood into pieces, so he wouldn't see my tears. Before he got closer, I ran into the kitchen, blew on the dying fire, and fed it some sticks. My hot tears continued to flow.

"Auma, you're tearing, that smoke is too much," Musa said. "Leave it for a minute." Musa reminded me so much of Baba in that moment.

"No, Musa, if I leave it, it'll be even harder to start. Don't worry, I'm fine."

"Okay," he said doubtfully. "I'll be back in a minute. I'm going to check on Mama."

I quickly wiped my tears away. I didn't want my siblings to think that I was already giving up on Mama. I had to be a brave woman. That was what Mama had taught me. She had always said that women had to be brave, because everyone needed their strength, and now the whole family was counting on me to have the courage to get things done.

I promised myself that I would.

By the time I got the fire going well, it was dark. I made haste to finish cooking the ugali for the evening meal. Since Dani had made a few sisal ropes that day and given them to a friend to sell at the market, there was a little bit of fish to go with the ugali. Even though I only got a few morsels, I savored every bite.

Over the past four months, Mama's skin had begun slowly developing lesions. She draped an old sweater around her, even during the midday sun, which covered most of the sores, but the ones on her face couldn't be hidden. She stopped leaving the house, and we each did all the chores—from firewood to water and market supplies. The only good news was that Akuku had stopped visiting. As Mama's condition worsened, her nighttime visitor had magically disappeared.

One evening Mama sent me to buy more oil at the market to rub on her knees and thighs. I returned as quickly as I could, hoping I could rub on the oil and still have a few minutes to collect my things for school and stretch my legs to prepare for the track tryouts. I dabbed the oil above her knee, then moved my hand upward.

"Don't touch beyond there," Mama snapped, stopping my hand at the same time.

"What is it, Mama?" I asked, startled.

"I have a . . . wound on this side of my thigh," she said, placing her hand over her leg.

"Let me see," I insisted. Part of her thigh looked burned, like her flesh had been set on fire.

"Oh, Mama, why haven't you gone to see the doctor?"

"Don't worry, I have medication for it already. It's just healing very slowly." I wondered how she could already have medication for something she'd developed after seeing the doctor. Not only was I scared and confused, but I was beginning to get angry with Mama.

I marched outside to Dani's hut. If I was going to battle Mama, I wasn't going to do it alone. I returned with Dani and showed her Mama's wound.

"You need to go to the hospital," Dani said decisively. I didn't always agree with her traditions and beliefs, but I was glad to have Dani on my side right now.

"You know we don't have money for the hospital," Mama protested. "We don't have anything that's worth a shilling . . . except the cow, and we can't sell that."

Dani turned to me. "Auma, tomorrow you must take that cow to the market and sell it."

I wondered why she wanted me to go instead of Juma or Musa. Tomorrow was the first day of the real track season. If I went to the market I would miss it. Besides, I was a girl. I couldn't remember any girls from our village taking cows to the market. For once I wished we had a tradition that would forbid my going. Something like, "It is a taboo for a girl to help sell a cow if she has a brother who is able."

But I sighed, accepting the responsibility. I was the one who'd brought Dani into this. Dani sent Juma to recruit one of our uncles, who would help me get a good price for the cow. I'd never bought or sold a cow before, so I had no idea how much money it would bring in. I only hoped it would be enough to cover Mama's hospital fees. And maybe there would be extra, to pay our school expenses.

I looked back at Mama, and all my other concerns suddenly seemed small. This is AIDS, I thought. All her symptoms point to it. I was not going to pretend that she couldn't be infected. I needed to brace myself for the worst—and do everything in my power to help her, no matter what the sacrifice.

◆◆◆

I watched Juma, Musa, and Baby leave the gate dressed in their school uniforms. I longed to be part of their group. But I was in charge now. Today, that meant selling a cow.

I tugged gently on the rope, guiding the cow toward my uncle's house. I'd miss track trials today, and I knew that several teachers would question my absence.

And what about next term's tuition? If Mama didn't get better, there was no way we'd have enough money to pay all of our school fees for the rest of the year. Juma and Musa were earning a little money working for the Bimas—enough for us to get by—but it wouldn't cover tuition.

With each thought, I felt hope slipping through my hands. Then I realized that it really was the rope slipping away, and the cow had wandered far ahead, eating grass along the side of the road. I was lucky she hadn't run away. I promised myself that I wouldn't lose focus again.

♦♦♦

Five hundred shillings kept Mama in the government hospital for an entire week. Nurses attended to her constantly, and the doctors gave her new medication. By day two, she was already showing signs of great progress.

The day she came home, I stayed home from school, and for once I didn't even mind. *Mama's better now*, I told myself. *That means this will be the last time I miss school.* I washed my uniform, happily singing, hopeful that God was healing Mama. I danced around the cooking fire while Juma eyed me suspiciously.

I was almost finished making supper when I heard a groan emerging from the choo.

I ran over and found Dani trying to hold Mama

up over the choo. I could see that my aging grandmother lacked the strength, and Mama had defecated all over her legs, missing the hole entirely. The stench was horrible.

I ran to get a cloth and the remaining bucket of water to wash Mama. I knew that I'd be staying home from school again the next day. My hopes were dashed. I felt like a fool for letting myself believe Mama could be cured.

I fought back tears as I gently washed my mother's legs. I looked from Dani to Mama—both had a look of hopelessness in their faces.

As the sun set that night, I felt like the sun had set in my life. My thoughts about the future fell away into darkness. Life had ended for me.

The next morning, I began a new routine. I woke up an hour before everyone and made thin porridge for my siblings to drink before school. As usual, the boys took off like a shot from the compound. As Baby trudged through the gate behind them, I had to remind her that running was the best way to make it there on time.

I recalled that when I was younger, nobody needed to tell me that. I just ran.

Baby is never going to be a runner, I thought. Watching her jog halfheartedly down the road, I felt a knot form in my throat. Maybe I could ask Sussie, our neighbor down the road, to have her younger siblings pass by our compound in the mornings and walk to school with Baby.

After my siblings were gone I was left alone in the quiet of the compound. It felt like a graveyard. Dani and Mama were still sleeping, and all I could hear was the cooing of the pigeons.

A winging bird landed in between the kitchen and the house, looking for something to eat. I stood there mindlessly staring, watching him peck a bit and leave. It was about the only excitement I'd had all morning.

I swept and tidied the kitchen and the front yard. I wanted to sing but had to restrain myself, because Mama was still asleep. I organized the pots and then started a fire to cook the porridge for Mama and Dani.

After cleaning up, I knew I had to make a trip to the stream alone. Even though we'd decided I shouldn't go there by myself, I now had no choice.

Without water I wouldn't be able to cook or bathe Mama, and some had to be boiled so it was safe to drink.

Along the way, I jumped at every sound I heard. The village was so quiet with the children at school. The dogs must still be asleep, and the cows still trying to wake up.

When I reached the stream's edge, there were several women there.

"Auma, why are you not at school?" Mama Karen asked.

I was fed up with village busybodies. I knew it was impolite, but I ignored her. I simply didn't answer. My life was none of her business. Plus, I knew I'd start crying if I had to talk about Mama's illness.

Maybe I was becoming like all the other Koromo people who didn't answer questions. What sort of person would I be by the time I reached Mama's age? So closed off that I wouldn't even be able to confide in those who loved me?

I didn't want to end up like that. Maybe I needed to think seriously about leaving Koromo—and not just until I could finish my education. For good. Everything I wanted—an education, a job that didn't end with marriage, a way to stop this terrible sickness—existed outside of Koromo, if it existed at all.

When I returned home from the stream, Dani was awake, but Mama was still sleeping. I boiled water. When she awoke, I wiped her sores, then helped her to the choo. I had an easy time because she had lost so much weight. Briefly I remembered Mr. Osogo saying that caregivers could be infected, but I pushed the thought back. Luckily I had no open wounds—and even if I did, would I leave my mother to take care of herself? No, I would just find something to cover my wound . . . I would do whatever it took to help Mama.

Mama seemed to have her courage back that day. She even managed to joke about her "beauty marks." We sat under the guava tree together for what seemed like the entire afternoon. I made sure she ate whatever was available. We talked about everything—relatives, church, school and track, and on and on. It felt like old times again, before we had so many worries.

"Mama, you know that I would like to go to secondary school and then university."

"Yes, I know. I've heard you talk about it many

times and I think you can. Your grades are quite good."

"Some of my classmates think it's just a dream."

Mama smiled. "Everything starts from a dream put into action. If you dream and do nothing about it, then it is just a dream. Staying in school is the first action toward reaching your future."

This sounded more like the Mama I remembered—the Mama who never gave up and always found a way to make our lives better somehow. Encouraged, I asked, "Mama, what did you want to be when you were growing up?"

"What do you mean?"

"I mean, what did you want to do when you finished school? As a career."

"Oh." Mama's face took on a faraway look. "I always wanted to be a teacher or a nurse. Those are the professions women are encouraged to get into, and I didn't mind. But I didn't have money for school fees, so I never went beyond Class Four. Already you've accomplished so much more than I ever did. Not only are you excelling in school, but you've become a first-rate nurse!"

I giggled at that. But then I felt foolish. Mama had still never talked in any detail about her condition. Maybe she thought I was too young to understand.

She didn't know that I'd more or less figured it out already. I wondered how she'd react if I just told her what I suspected. Maybe then she'd see how old I really was.

I realized I was going to have to be the adult, to ask questions and demand answers.

"Being the nurse, I need to ask you—do you know what you're really suffering from?"

"Not really. One day it's my skin, the next it's my stomach. I think we just need to let the medications do what they're meant to do. You worry too much, Auma. I'll be fine. The world is tough, and we all have to be brave in spite of such hard times."

"I know," I whispered, nodding. I felt a lump in my throat. How could I ever find a cure for this disease if I couldn't even talk to Mama about it?

When the other children returned, I asked her if I could run to Abeth's for a few minutes to check on homework.

Abeth had become my lifeline since Mama became sick. These days, we had more in common than ever. We supported each other like sisters. I ran all the way to her compound, thinking I might get there before she returned from school. To my surprise, she was already home.

"I've been waiting for you," Abeth said.

I wrinkled my forehead. "How did you know I'd be coming?"

"You wouldn't have been missing school and track unless it was serious," she said, then quietly added, "and I know what serious is." I heard her voice fighting hard not to cry.

"Abeth," I said, "what would I do if . . ." The words stuck in my throat.

"Look at me," said Abeth, swallowing. "How am I doing? You'll be fine."

"Thanks, Abeth. I don't know what I'd do without you."

She reached out and took my hand. "What can I do to help?"

"I need you to bring me my books and homework every day that I miss school. I'm going to ask the principal to excuse me from dawn study hours and let me do my work from home. I'll get Mrs. Okumu to convince him if I can't."

She nodded. "What about track?"

"I'll talk to Mr. Ouma and convince him to let me on the team even though I missed trials. I'll promise that I won't miss any of the track meets. I can still make my dream come true."

"Oh, Auma," she sighed, suddenly weary. "What dreams can girls like us really have?"

"Abeth, think about it. If I get a scholarship to a secondary school and do well there, I can become a doctor someday. And then, I'll find a way to prevent people from getting this disease. That's my dream." I closed my eyes, tilting my face to the sky, as if I were seeking guidance from above.

"And you can have dreams too," I added. "We just need to continue with our education, so we can't get married too early. We both know that as soon as we quit school, some man will come and pay a bride price, and then before you know it we'll be having babies."

"Listen to yourself, Auma." Abeth's voice was impatient, almost cold. "You're talking about *us* finding a way. I've learned not to waste so much time on dreams. It hurts when they don't work out. Besides, there's nothing wrong with being a wife or a mother. There can be happiness in that kind of life too."

"Don't try to change my mind, Abeth. I know what I'm talking about. I want to find prevention for this disease that killed your parents and my father. You know—AIDS."

For the first time, I said the word out loud. Even if the rest of Koromo wasn't ready to say it, I would be. After all, I was going to be the one to stop it.

Something in Abeth seemed to snap. "Eeee! How come the wazungu in Europe and America haven't found prevention?" she shouted. "They're dying too, remember? Mr. Osogo told us. So what makes you think *you* will find prevention before the knowledgeable wazungu? You think you're so smart, huh?"

"Brains have nothing to do with what color your skin is," I retorted. "Listen to yourself, Abeth. I don't care about the whites. I care about us. I care about Koromo. Our homes smell like death. Our village will soon be filled with only children. Why is it so wrong to want something better?" My chest heaved. I held my breath to keep from sobbing.

Abeth's cheeks were now wet with tears. "Forgive me, Auma. Sometimes—sometimes I get jealous of you. Even now, you're going through what I've gone through and you're stronger. You have hope. You have faith. Where does it come from?"

I held my friend in my arms. Where *did* my strength come from? I looked up at the heavens, wondering if the answer was there.

I had no explanation for why I still believed good things were possible. But I did know that talking openly about this disease had been a relief. I had finally accepted what was killing my people—even if I didn't know how to stop it. Yet.

If Abeth saw faith in me, I had to see it in myself. I owed it to her, and to God who created me, to be the miracle I was born to be.

CHAPTER 18

"Auma, Auma, get up, you'll all be late to school if you don't wake up right now!"

Mama's voice interrupted my dreams. What was she doing up before me? Had I slept too late?

I jumped to my feet. This was still my usual way of waking up, no matter how tired I was. "Are you feeling any better, Mama?" I asked, peering through the curtain that hung in the doorway to my mother's bedroom.

"Don't worry, I'm fine—now move fast. You don't have much time left," Mama urged me. "Wake Baby up right now. And make sure you leave some porridge and water for me when you leave for school."

I was surprised and confused. I hadn't been able to go to school for a couple of weeks, and Mama hadn't woken up this early in a long time. I didn't argue, though. I knew how quickly things could turn around, so I woke up my sister and brothers, then got dressed.

The sun was peeping on the horizon, making the dry leaves look golden brown. I hurried to complete my early morning chores, cleaning the kitchen from last evening's cooking, washing the dishes, and starting a fire. I hurried back and forth between the kitchen and the house, making sure everyone was on task.

Juma's job was to sweep the dirt immediately in front of the house. Clouds of dirt swirled as he vigorously swept, trying to finish quickly.

"Sprinkle water, please," I reminded him as I always did. It seemed that in his mind dirt was as good to breathe in as clean air was.

"Baby, put on your uniform, and Musa, find your shirt, or you'll be late."

I was getting better at taking charge, but today, with Mama acting so much stronger, maybe I wasn't going to have to do that as much. Maybe I'd been wrong about Mama's illness. I felt a surge of energy at the prospect. I decided to boil the last bit of cassava for breakfast, just to celebrate. I'd had enough thin porridge to last a lifetime. I inhaled the smell as it began to boil.

Mama mustered enough energy to walk to the kitchen. "What are you doing, Auma?!" she scolded, looking at the cooking pot with surprise.

"Cooking cassava for breakfast," I answered, dumbfounded.

"Auma, do you even realize how long this cassava will need to boil?" She snatched the spoon from my hand and let out a grunt.

I felt stupid. I had completely forgotten that cassava takes three times as long to boil as millet porridge. I hadn't cooked the cassava the night before, and there was no way it would be ready in time—if we didn't want a spanking for getting to school late.

"Juma, please move faster," I called. I could already feel the backs of my legs stinging, imagining the caning we would get.

We headed to school with empty bellies. I should have just made porridge and saved my ambition for something else, like track or schoolwork. By the time we got to school, the morning assembly was almost over. We'd missed the class lineup, singing the national anthem, and reciting the pledge. The headmaster was finishing the last announcement as we reached the school gate.

Mr. Ouma waited by the gate to punish latecomers. He held his patrol stick, batting and smacking it into his palm while giving students "the eye."

My heart sank when I saw him smiling. There was no way to avoid a caning. He was probably especially angry with me, for missing the first district track meet the week before: KaPeter Primary had lost.

"Why are you late?" he demanded.

I opened my mouth but no words came out. Besides, excuses would mean nothing to him. Like all the other teachers, he refused to give orphans any special considerations.

Juma, Musa, and Baby hid behind me.

"Sir, we'll never be late again," I finally managed, my voice quivering with fear. I closed my eyes, ready for whatever Mr. Ouma was going to do to me, knowing the pain would be brief.

Instead I heard Baby cry out, and I opened my eyes. Mr. Ouma was moving toward her. I stepped closer to her.

"Hey, little girl, what's your name?" Mr. Ouma said, sounding like a lion purring to its dinner.

"My . . . my name is Baby," she stuttered, sniffling.

"Oh baby, baby, what is your school name?" He was taunting her, and I could feel my fists tighten into a ball. Whatever he was going to dish out to my brothers and sister, I had to stand by and watch. Here was one situation where I could not take charge.

"My name is Mary," she said as she wiped at her tears.

"Now listen, Mary, you can never get to school late again. Otherwise you'll feel this pain again," he said as he struck her legs with the stick. Caught off guard, Baby screeched like a kitten whose tail had been stepped on.

"Run to class quickly," her tormenter shouted, laughing. She ran as fast as her little legs could go, crying the entire way.

"Next!" He pointed his stick at Musa.

Musa moved forward. *Whack, whack, whack!* Then off he ran.

Juma stepped forward next and received three whacks. Now it was my turn.

Mr. Ouma glared at me. "Class Eight students are not supposed to ever come late to school. You should have been here at dawn."

The principal had given me permission to miss the study hour as long as I still got my work done, but I knew better than to say so to Mr. Ouma. He was obviously determined to punish me no matter what.

Mr. Ouma hit me harder than the others. I bit my lip and kept my eyes open, determined not to be defeated.

I walked to class, calves throbbing, but managing not to limp. I wouldn't give him the satisfaction of knowing how badly he'd hurt me.

In class, I struggled to concentrate. My legs throbbed with pain. At lunch, I hid around the corner of the building and smeared wet clay on my bruises, the way Dani had taught me to do when I was little. The clay felt cold for a while, but after some time it baked and crusted on my legs, pinching my skin.

As soon as Mrs. Okumu arrived to teach language, I forced my mind back to class. I realized it had been a long time since I borrowed a book for the weekend. This morning Mrs. Okumu discussed the short story we'd read the day before: "The Fattening Rooms of Calabar." She asked questions and expected participation from everyone, but found that only a handful of us could remember the story. Abeth had brought me the story, but I hadn't had time to read it, so I was relieved when Mrs. Okumu told us to reread it right now.

The story was about how the West African girls of Calabar were fattened in order to prepare them for marriage. I liked the idea of the plentiful food. But the problem was that the girls had no choice about when and how much to eat. They were forced to eat all day long. I was glad this wasn't part of our culture—though some of our traditions made me just as uneasy.

I finished the story well before the silent reading time was up. As I waited on my classmates, I found myself thinking of Mama and her illness. How her unpredictable condition was affecting everything. I was exhausted just trying to keep up. Of course, it wasn't her fault, but I didn't see how we could go on like this much longer.

CHAPTER 19

If Mama was going to get well, something had to be done immediately. The medications from the hospital weren't helping enough. I needed to find someone who could give her the best medicine. Which meant finding an adult who would talk to me openly about the alternatives.

It had been more than a year since I first heard the gossip about the medicine man. I needed to know if people still believed that he could cure AIDS. If he'd stopped having success with his patients, consulting him would be a waste of my time.

Since Mama Karen knew everyone's business and a lot more, I decided to go talk to her. For the first time in my life, I actively sought her out at the market, where she had a vegetable stall.

"Good afternoon," I greeted her, hoping she

wouldn't raise her voice and draw the attention of everyone around us.

"How are you, young lady? What can I do for you? How is your grandmother?" Mama Karen asked loudly.

Please, Lord, I prayed, *make her soften her voice.* I thought about turning around and running.

"Fine, thank you," I heard myself saying. "I . . . I'd like to buy some vegetables from you. My mother will pay you later."

As Mama Karen consented and wrapped up the food, I bent close to her and whispered, "May I ask you a question?"

"Why yes," she whispered back, finally picking up on the need for discretion.

"About this illness that's going around in the village . . ."

"Yes, my child."

"Do you know where someone can get treatment?"

"Oh, no! Do you have it too? Auma, what have you been doing?" She held her hand to her chest, eyeing me with suspicion.

"No, no. I just want to know if there's hope for the infected people."

"Why does it concern you?"

Was it possible that no gossip about Mama had reached Mama Karen's ears? Maybe she was just pretending ignorance. I knew all too well that Koromo was too small a place for someone to get sick without people noticing—especially Mama Karen. But I couldn't let that bother me now. I had to do whatever I could to help Mama.

"Ahh . . . I just wanted to know because we were given a homework assignment at school to ask people if they knew about any kind of treatment."

"My girl, what you're asking me is very unusual. I've never been asked such a question by a child."

I gave her a fake smile but prayed that she would say something useful. Instead she turned her attention to some women who'd come to buy vegetables from her. I stood there waiting, wondering what to do. At least she had kept her voice down while we talked. If she wouldn't help me, I could walk away as if nothing happened.

"If you're not sure, then I should be going," I finally said, turning to leave.

"Just a minute." Mama Karen gestured for me to lean in closer to her. She whispered in my ear, "They say that Pino, the medicine man, does a good job. Quite a few people have been cured after visiting him."

"What about payment?" I asked.

"He doesn't charge much. Now go! And don't tell a soul that Mama Karen told you that."

I left without looking back. My heart was beating fast. I couldn't believe I'd been bold enough to ask Mama Karen about the medicine man. Now I had a confirmation that he was still successfully treating AIDS patients. And now that I had this information, I had to decide whether to use it.

♦♦♦

That night, standing next to Mama's bed, I wondered whether there was any hope at all. She was wasting away again—more quickly, it seemed. She had improved a little when I'd been with her all day long, but now that I'd gone back to school, her health had deteriorated once more.

"Mama."

"Yes?" Her voice sounded far off.

"I want to take you outside so you can feel the warmth of the sun. It's five o'clock and the sun is soft and nice."

"No, Auma, I can't get up, I don't have the energy."

"I can help you get up."

"I don't think you can, so why bother?" These days, Mama's misery could make her stubborn. If it were up to her, she'd never leave her bed. It was my job to make sure she didn't forget what it was like to be alive.

"Musa, come help me!" I called.

Together we lifted Mama out of bed, walked her to the veranda, and helped her sit. She looked like a skeleton. We would have taken her to the hospital, but the money from selling the cow was long gone. I headed into the kitchen and started boiling porridge for supper. I made sure Baby watched me—it was time for her to start learning to cook. Through the tiny kitchen window, I called to the boys, "Dinner's in an hour. Get started on your homework while you wait." I was tired of taking charge, but I knew it was my duty. If I didn't make sure my brothers were doing their schoolwork, no one would.

"Auma, why is Mama always sick?" Baby asked in a small voice.

I bit my lip. "Baby, she has a sickness that's worse than typhoid and malaria combined. She's trying her best to stay strong, but it's not easy."

"When will she get well?"

"I don't know. We must keep praying." I felt just like the adults who'd refused to be open with me. But I couldn't bring myself to tell Baby that Mama had a disease with no cure—that she was probably dying. It would be too much for her to take.

No doubt that was why Mama wouldn't share more information with me. But I wasn't Baby's age. I could understand and deal with the truth.

In my heart I knew Mama wasn't getting any better. Once again the shadow of death seemed to have settled over our house. *Don't despair*, I told myself firmly. Hope was all I had to keep the flame in me from dying. It was certainly flickering now.

After about ten minutes of sitting out on the veranda, Mama needed to lie down. I lowered her onto our mat as the sun slowly dropped behind the hills, like a big, red, rolling ball. Its bright orange light poured through the open door, illuminating the inside of our house. That meant I could see enough to change Mama's bedsheets.

"Okay, Mama, the sun has set. I'll take you in."

"Thank you, Auma. It was a beautiful sunset. It's great to see such a beautiful sunset when your life is setting." Tears were streaming down her cheeks.

I could feel my heart splintering, but I focused on helping her get back into the bedroom. I didn't want the younger children to see Mama this way.

After I'd gently lowered her onto her bed, I sat on the chair next to her in the now-darkened room. She tried to control her sobs, but her body was quaking so hard that the bed shook. Seeing Mama like that, I knew I was going to cry too. I didn't want to go outside because I was afraid the others would see my tears and ask questions—those questions that were unbearably hard to answer, to even think about. So I just stayed with Mama and cried softly with her until she stopped.

My thoughts went to Baba. He had died almost six months ago, but it felt like yesterday. I remembered thinking he was so thin he looked like he was nothing but skin over bones, and had reached the point where he couldn't eat on his own, but had to be fed like a baby.

As I looked at Mama, I realized she had become like that. At this point all I wanted was a confirmation from her that she had AIDS, yet I couldn't muster the courage to ask. Part of me felt that it wasn't fair to ask her to admit it. She was already suffering. And speaking the name wouldn't change what was happening to her. Yet I felt that Mama telling me would bring closure. I hoped the right time would come.

When I stepped out of the bedroom, Juma looked up from the kerosene lantern he was holding. "Dinner's about ready," I said. "Can you get some water for Mama to wash her hands, and then take Dani's food over to her?"

"Sure, just as soon as I finish with this."

"Thanks," I said. "And thanks for taking care of the lantern."

"No problem." I stopped and turned around. That expression reminded me of Baba.

I stood there for a moment as Juma went back to making sure the lamp was well lit. He started cleaning it, exactly as Baba had taught him. He wiped the base and the top, and then put it on the lamp stand, just like old times, when he and Baba would light all the lanterns together.

There was something very special about the process. Learning to clean the kerosene lantern had taken Juma a long time. He never seemed to get it as clean as our father wanted. But since he had started doing it himself, he had mastered it. When the lantern was lit, the room sparkled.

I took some ugali and a few scarce vegetables to my mother. A moment later Juma came in with a plastic bowl filled with water.

I was so thankful that most of the time my brothers were willing to help out. So many boys were rowdy and thoughtless, even rude. Juma and Musa had inherited the best of Baba—his willingness to lend a hand whenever it was needed.

That night Mama ate all her food and went to sleep as soon as she had cleaned her hands. She slept so soundly that I feared the worst. I put my ear next to her mouth to make sure she was breathing. I stayed there for a long time.

With each breath, the courage to do something built inside me. I knew I had to fight for Mama. I had to try everything—even what she never tried for Baba.

CHAPTER 20

The next morning, I told my siblings to go ahead, that I would catch up with them. I sprinted the quarter mile to Abeth's house faster than I can remember ever running before. The thorny bushes along the path seemed to come alive as I passed, with creatures scurrying away from the sound of my feet thumping on the rocky path. In Koromo, rocks seem to multiply like rodents, but I leaped over them, causing birds to take flight around me. The noisy flight of the pigeons and weaver birds made me feel like I was moving even faster. I only slowed down when I reached the entrance to Abeth's compound.

"Abeth!" I yelled.

"Coming!" she responded, stepping out of her grandmother's hut, her bag hanging over her shoulder. She pulled the wooden door shut, securing it with the metal latch. "What are you doing here?"

"I need to talk to you before school. Come on." As we started walking, I said in a low voice, "Mama Karen told me that the medicine man has a cure for AIDS. We need to go to him and get it."

The more I said it, the more comfortable I became with the word.

"What?! I'm not going to any medicine man. And call it Slim, please . . . if you even have to call it something out loud."

"Abeth, it's my mother," I pleaded.

"If she wants his help, she'll have to go see him herself! She shouldn't be asking us."

"She doesn't have the strength to go on her own. We have to try, please."

"Have you ever heard of children going to the medicine man alone?" she said.

"We're not children anymore, Abeth. And I know it sounds crazy, but my mother deserves my best effort."

"You're talking about being the first young people to approach that man alone. Do you realize how dangerous that is? The man has crazy people in his compound. People say there are evil powers in there. We don't know what we'd be walking into."

"I don't believe that Pino is dangerous, Abeth. And if it turns out he is, I'll get you out of there safely." I was making shaky promises, but I was desperate. "We have our legs," I added. "If we need to get out of there fast, we can run."

Abeth was quiet for some time before responding.

"How much have you heard about him?"

I shrugged. "I've heard a few different things. Some are really strange, but not scary. During Baba's funeral, I heard the women say that the medicine man could heal anything, even though his methods are . . . unusual."

"Yes, I know," Abeth said, quietly.

I eyed her suspiciously. "So *you* know something?"

"When I was little, my mother took me with her to check on her cousin who had lost his mind and was being treated there."

"Really? You said we'd be the first children to go!" My mouth hung wide open. I couldn't believe Abeth had never told me she'd seen the medicine man before.

"And we still would be the first without parents. I can't remember much, but . . ."

Abeth shivered, even though the morning was already hot. "I do remember that there were all sorts of patients in his compound. Some were basking in the morning sun. Others were helping with the chores. One man sat by a hut staring into the sky. And a young man rushed to us thinking we were his parents who had come to take him home." Abeth swallowed hard, then continued. Her eyes had a far-away look, as if she was going into a trance.

"The scariest place was the medicine man's hut. It was half dark inside. There was a fire glowing strangely on one side."

"You actually went into the hut?" I asked, stopping in my tracks.

Abeth nodded. "Things were hanging every-where, from the roof and walls. I saw a deer head with gnarled horns, dried-up snakeskins, roots, twigs, tree barks. There were cans, tins, all sorts of things strewn all over the floor. I saw a live serpent crawling up the wall just before it vanished."

"And Pino himself?"

She shuddered. "His face was in shadows, at least the way I remember it. But I remember he was using a chameleon to treat a patient. He made small cuts on the man's body and had the chameleon lick the patient's blood."

Chameleons were rare creatures in our part of the world, but that was hardly the strangest thing about

Abeth's story. "What happened to your cousin? The one who went there for treatment?"

"I think she got better for a while, but I haven't seen her in years, so I don't know if it lasted." Abeth paused. "Do you still want to go?"

I hesitated. Why were my options always so grim? "I have to try."

◆◆◆

On Sunday morning the sun rose hot and bright. Sunday was usually a quiet day in Koromo. Some people stayed home and relaxed, while others went to church. I realized it had been a long time since we'd been to church. Without Mama dragging us there, we'd forgotten. Maybe we'd forgotten about God entirely. I said a quick prayer for forgiveness. Then I thanked God for what I still had, before asking Him to protect me that day. I needed His protection as much as ever.

By eleven o'clock I could hear drumming and singing coming from the church. It echoed off the hills surrounding Koromo. My steps were in rhythm with the *thum-titi-thum* as I hurried toward Abeth's home. Dani and my siblings assumed we were going to collect firewood with the other girls, as usual. No one knew about our planned detour to visit the medicine man.

On the way to Abeth's, I watched some neighbors tending their crops. The peanut harvest was in progress. Judging by the air's nutty smell and the occasional pile of cracked shells lining the path, I could see that despite the short rains, this year's harvest was decent. *A sign of hope*, I thought, grateful for anything to get my mind off what I was about to do.

Abeth met me at the door. Inside, her dani was sitting in her usual chair. I greeted her as brightly as I could manage.

"Good morning, Auma," she said, reaching for her walking stick. She was the kindest grandmother I had ever met—not like mine, who only reached for her walking stick when she was about to hit you with it.

"Make sure you get back when the sun is still high," Abeth's grandmother reminded her.

"We will," we chorused, locking eyes nervously.

We set out armed with small *pangas*—cutlasses for cutting wood—and ropes tied around our waists for tying our woodpiles. We would make more ropes out of the wild sisal plants if we needed to.

As soon as we had walked far into the bush

where it would be difficult for anyone to hear us, I reminded Abeth that we needed to work fast. That way, once we'd collected plenty of wood, we'd be able to go on our mission and still get home on time.

We diligently went to work, not taking a moment to chat with any of the other girls. Once we had gathered a heap of wood, we camouflaged it under some leafy branches.

I wiped the sweat from my forehead, amazed we had finished the chore so quickly. "Okay, let's go," I huffed.

Abeth and I sneaked out of the forest and headed toward the medicine man's compound before the other girls realized we were gone. Ten minutes later, we approached the only entrance to the place. Two towering eucalyptus trees guarded each side of the opening. The compound was fenced by tightly planted and trimmed trees. We peered through the spaces and counted several round grass-thatched huts inside the compound.

We tiptoed toward the entrance and paused, looking at each other with dread, as if it were the last time we might see each other's faces. If anything happened to us, I would be to blame. I was the one who had insisted we go. All the same, Abeth boldly took the lead, heading toward the circular hut at the center of the compound.

"Abeth," I whispered, "those people are watching us."

"Shhhh, we just need to find the medicine man."

"Hello, girls," a tall, skinny lady called in greeting as she walked out of one of the huts. Unlike most women in the village, who cut their hair short or wore head wraps, she had long, braided hair.

"Have you been sent?" she asked.

Abeth hesitated and then said, "Yes. We would like to talk to the medicine man. Where is he?"

"What is it that you need?" she asked politely. "I'm his wife and can also help you, unless you need treatment."

Something was different about the way the woman spoke. I wondered if she had come here from another part of Kenya, or even another country in Africa. I'd heard that some medicine men got their training in Tanzania. Perhaps this woman had been there too. She might know many worldly things if she had lived outside of Koromo. But still, she wasn't the medicine man.

"We've come to speak to the medicine man," I said. "My mother needs treatment."

"Oh, in that case you have to see him. Wait here, I'll go and find out if he can see you," she said, and walked into his hut.

After a few minutes she emerged and motioned with one cupped hand for us to come forward.

We took long, quick strides toward the hut, fearing that something would stop us before we got to the door.

"Come in," a deep male voice called from within.

We stepped through the doorway. It took a few seconds for our eyes to adjust to the dimness of the hut, which didn't have a single window. That made me nervous. I could feel my armpits and palms sweating already.

The man was sitting near a smoldering fire, holding a calabash of porridge.

"What brings you here?" His voice was surprisingly gentle.

Before we could answer, something skittered sharply on the wall right above the medicine man's head: a rough, scaly lizard climbing the wall to avoid a chameleon. I drew back, holding my breath, my attention on the chameleon rather than the lizard. I was astonished and terrified that this rare creature was so close to where I was standing. My eyes began to sweep the whole hut. Just as Abeth had remembered, there were charms and roots hanging everywhere from the roof and the walls. On the floor by the far wall opposite the entrance, I saw a still body that was covered with a blanket. I wondered whether the person was alive. As if in response to my question, the body stirred and groaned, and then went limp again.

I inhaled deeply and looked straight ahead.

"My mother is sick, sir," I said, trying to ignore my haunting surroundings. "Can you find some herbs for her?"

"What is she suffering from?"

I hesitated. Now that we were here, I wasn't at all sure I could trust this man. "I don't know . . ."

"Yesss you do, child," he hissed.

I gulped.

"Can you describe her symptoms?" he continued in a gentler voice.

"She's very thin. She doesn't eat much. Someone has to help her to the choo. She has sores on most parts of her body, and a large one on her thigh." I hoped this answer wouldn't earn me another hiss.

His eyes remained on us as he moved the calabash toward his mouth to sip some porridge. He sort of gargled it, still not breaking eye contact.

"I can't treat your mother. She has waited too long."

My knees gave out, and I almost fell. Quickly I straightened. *Focus, Auma.* This might be the only chance I had left to save my mother's health.

"I've been told that you're the best. Could you at least give her something to help her feel better? Please."

"Now young lady, where do you get this boldness? I have never in my life seen two young and fertile girls like you come to seek my help."

"Sir, is something wrong with what we're doing?"

"Well, yes and no." He considered. "It is very dangerous to come to such a place and see all these things and just walk away. How do I know what you will tell others about me? There are those who want me banished, you know." He stopped, moving his gaze from my eyes to Abeth's. "The medicine man chooses how you fare from here," he said.

Suddenly, my heart started racing. Was he going to put some spell on us to keep us from leaving? Was he afraid we would spread lies about what we'd seen here, out of resentment that he'd refused to help Mama?

I desperately searched for the right words. "Sir, I mean no disrespect. I'm just trying to help my mother. You're not going to do something bad to us just because we came here, are you?"

The medicine man laughed loudly, ending with a ridiculous snort. "Fear not, my children. You," he pointed at me, "you speak like a determined and brave girl. Next time someone you know is sick, make sure you bring the sick one to me. Then I can try some treatments, if the illness hasn't progressed too far. Oh," he added, lowering his pitch to sound eerily serious, "and don't lie about having an appointment."

Just then, the body in the blanket awoke, stood, and shuffled toward us. Abeth and I took our cue and backed out of the hut as fast as we could. We sprinted out of the compound, all the way back to where we'd left our firewood. Out of breath and shaking, we stared at each other, wondering what had just happened.

"I'm so glad we got out of there fast," Abeth finally said. "He almost cursed us!"

"I don't think he really would've cursed us. I think he was just trying to scare us because we didn't have any money to pay him for his advice." Anger rippled through me. "When I become a doctor, I'll *never* bully someone like that."

I felt betrayed. I wouldn't get a chance to help Mama. I wondered if God had a hand in this. Maybe God hadn't wanted me to go there. Maybe I should have gone to see the pastor instead. I felt a surge of shame. I hadn't been a very faithful Christian lately. Why couldn't I just believe in God the way I wanted to, and pray and worship the way God seemed to want? What did I have to do for God to listen?

"If you can hear me now, God, give me the strength to do whatever I'm supposed to do!" I shouted at the sky, turning in circles. Abeth put her arm around my neck. I felt calmer and stopped turning. I let my head rest on her arm.

"Here, I'll carry the bigger load." Abeth scooped up the heavier pile of firewood and added dryly, "I feel moved to take the burden off you today."

I smiled appreciatively. Looking at my friend, who admittedly didn't believe much of the Bible, I felt at peace with what had just happened. God hadn't answered me in the way I wanted, but for the moment, I'd been given the strength to keep going.

CHAPTER 21

"Auma, I want you back here promptly after school." Dani's forehead seemed to have accumulated a million wrinkles overnight. "Your mother needs more help than I can handle."

"Okay, Dani. You know, I can stay home if you want me to." I squinted my eyes and held my breath. Today was the district track meet, and I would be dismissed from class early to participate. Officers from the district and possibly the provincial office would be on the sidelines. If I won today, there was the chance that one might take interest in me. Getting an officer to notice me was my best chance of being offered a running scholarship for secondary school.

I waited for Dani's answer.

"No, I know today is an important day for you. I'll manage until you get home. But be back here as soon as you can." I thanked Dani and dashed off, just in case she might change her mind. Her face had looked as stern and tired as always, but as the rising sun's rays hit her face, her eyes seemed softer this morning.

◆◆◆

The moment the principal announced that the track team was dismissed, I sprinted out of the classroom. Today, I was going to prove that I had more reasons to run than anyone else on the team. My entire future depended on this race.

Students from Pala, Kogeno, and other primary schools in the district were already filing in onto the freshly groomed track. Standing near the finish line was a man holding a clipboard with the Kenyan national flag on the underside. He must be a scout from a prestigious provincial high school. Another man, whom I recognized as a teacher from a less respected nearby high school, was talking to him.

As I stretched, I kept a close eye on them. At one point they both looked in my direction. Boldly, I lifted my hand and waved.

"Who are you waving at?" Abeth turned, squinting in the sun. "Is that—Yes! It is!" She giggled excitedly.

When we finished stretching we rushed to the registration table.

"Name, please?" asked the secretary, without even looking up from her clipboard.

"Auma Onyango, KaPeter Primary School," I said with pride. The woman looked up at me.

"So you're the one everyone's been talking about? Don't disappoint them today, Auma." She smiled and handed me a number to pin to my shirt.

I caught Mr. Ouma's eye, and he raised his fist as if to cheer me on. I knew he expected me to win my races today, and help our school earn another trophy. I threw the gesture back at him, to confirm that I was going to win. I believed it wholeheartedly.

The first race for the day was the relay, which would be followed by the 400-meter dash and the 100-meter dash.

Our team easily won the relay. Next came the 400 meters. Like lightning it was over—I had won, followed by Abeth. That left only one more race.

"For the 100-meter race, Heat One, girls, please, on your mark," the voice called over the loudspeaker. Abeth and I took our places in lanes three and four. My heart was beating wildly. I took in a deep breath and exhaled loudly.

By now it was difficult to concentrate with all the cheering from the spectators. I could tell that the scouts were watching me closely. Assuming I ran well in this last race, they'd want to talk to me afterward. As I lined up with the rest of my team, I tried to imagine what they would say to me—what they would tell me about their high schools, whether they would offer me a scholarship outright or encourage me to fill out some kind of application . . .

As I crouched over my mark, I saw a small figure running and flailing its arms near the finish line. I could see it was a boy in uniform.

Musa. Signaling to me. For him to even be here, he would've had to skip school. My heart jumped into my throat.

Something was wrong.

"Get set," the announcer called.

Tears rushed to the corners of my eyes. My fantasies about talking to the secondary school scouts, hearing their praise and getting their advice, evaporated. Couldn't Dani have waited another thirty seconds to summon me home . . . or . . .

"Go!"

I raced toward Musa with all the strength my legs had in them. The whole world began to disappear around me. I couldn't see or hear anything clearly. A haze blurred every figure. In front of me was the face of my mother.

I blazed past the finish line and kept going without missing a step.

"Musa, let's go!" I shouted over my shoulder. I didn't care that I had won all my races, that my performance had surely won the respect of Mr. Ouma and the secondary school scouts, or that everyone would be cheering for me in that moment—a moment I could've had all to myself if I wanted. If my life had been different.

I sprinted right past the crowds and through the gate. I turned once to make sure Musa could keep up. "What's happened?" I called to him as we ran.

"Dani says Mama's fading fast."

In Musa's determined face, all I could see was Baba's nose and eyes. Baba, who'd cared so much for us.

Baba, who'd let Mama down. He couldn't have known what would happen, how we would all suffer because of his actions. It would break his heart to see us now.

My heart was breaking too. But my legs carried me toward home with greater purpose than ever before.

CHAPTER 22

I stepped into the house as quietly as I could, which wasn't very quiet at all. I was completely out of breath. I could hear Juma and Baby outside behind the house. Through the back door I could see Baby playing in the dirt. Dani was in the sitting room, resting her chin on her walking stick. I could see her eyes were wet. Panic passed through my body.

I rushed into Mama's room and saw Mama Benta sitting there quietly. Tears welled up in my eyes. Our neighbor's offer to help had been sincere. Here she was, helping our family again—and this time, I hadn't even asked. I smiled and nodded at her to show my gratitude.

I reached out to open the only tiny window in the bedroom. "Mama, are you awake?"

"Yes," came her hoarse voice.

"How was your day?" I asked.

"I am here," she answered, faintly.

"Can I bring you something?"

"No—help your brothers make dinner, then come back later when Mama Benta has to go. I'll need my bath then."

I found the boys in the kitchen, shucking corn. Not corn from our garden: we always took that to the posho mill for grinding into flour. Fresh corn on the cob was expensive. I figured Mama Benta had something to do with this.

As the boys washed the corn, I washed some beans, put them into a clay pot with water, and set them over the fire. Later, I would add in the corn. With the clay pot, the food would be ready in an hour, so we would eat just after sundown. With Mama Benta around while it was still light, I might have time to do my homework before giving Mama her bath.

National exams were coming up in November, just a few months away, and I felt completely unprepared for them. Then again, if I couldn't get a track scholarship to pay for high school, what was the point of worrying about the exams? I'd blown my chance to speak to the scouts by running off this evening, leaving the other runners to claim their attention.

Maybe I could explain to Mr. Ouma why I left so quickly, and he could let the scouts know. My future schooling depended on their help.

I got my books and sat on the veranda to work in the light before the sunset. The math problems were easy, which slightly cheered me up. At this rate, I figured I'd get everything done in less than thirty minutes and might even have time to read a book for fun.

Before I finished the last math problem, Mama called me.

I jumped to my feet and ran inside.

"Please give me my bath now, I'm hot," she said, breathing hard and noisily.

I filled a plastic basin with water and grabbed a towel. I knew Mama wasn't going to make it to the choo and that I would be giving her a bed-bath, as usual. As I dampened a corner of the towel and carefully swabbed her thighs—being especially careful with the sores—I thought of everything that had happened since morning. Since last year.

Mama didn't have long. Days, maybe a week or two at the most. If ever there was a time to say what was unsaid between us, this was it. After everything we'd been through together, surely we could manage to speak the truth.

Courage swelled from my feet to my fingertips. "Mama, is it true that you have . . . AIDS?"

She was quiet for a long moment.

"Yes, Auma." She opened her mouth as if she wanted to say more, but then closed it and sighed.

"Why did you keep it a secret from me?"

"Auma, I'm not a bad person. I know what people say about us, about the ones who get sick. A lot of what people say isn't true. You have to believe me . . ."

"Of course I believe you, Mama. I know you did nothing wrong."

She looked directly in my eyes. "Auma, I made the mistake of thinking you were too young to know. But listen carefully now. What people don't know is just as harmful. Promise you'll always be brave enough to ask about anything you need to know."

Once again, Mama turned it all around. She found a way to make me feel valued. She spoke as if my future depended on the answers to my questions. I felt passion and vigor running back through me.

As I continued bathing her, she spoke more clearly than I had heard in a long time.

"When your father went to work in the city, he had another woman there. He didn't tell me until it was too late. Even before he was gone, I feared this was coming."

Suddenly, a wave of rage surged through me. It felt like my blood was boiling. Baba was the only man I'd ever completely trusted. He'd let us down. He'd been unfaithful to Mama. And he hadn't just ruined his own health—he'd harmed Mama and put our whole family in jeopardy.

I heard a clanging from the kitchen, and thought of Juma and Musa. Every time I looked at them, I was reminded more of Baba. Would they, too, some-day disappoint me—or their wives?

"Your father was a good man. But this world is very sinful. I knew the day he left that a man in the city without his family wasn't a good thing. All the same, we needed money to survive, to send all of you to school, so what was I supposed to do?"

I felt a surge of guilt for loving school so much. "Mama, don't blame yourself for what happened."

"I didn't know your father had the disease until the time I took him to the hospital to get checked, and the doctor said he had . . . he had . . . it." Even Mama couldn't repeat the name of it. "Your father had hidden it from me the whole time, but when there was no denying it, he told me everything in the doctor's office. I'd never seen a man cry so many tears, Auma."

Mama was sobbing. I used the towel to wipe her face, hoping the coolness would calm her.

"God will forgive me, I think," she said, and turned her head away.

"Mama, you haven't done anything wrong!"

I stopped washing her and straightened up. I wondered if she felt guilty about getting involved with Akuku. He never came around anymore, and in truth I'd almost forgotten about him. I certainly didn't blame Mama for whatever arrangement he'd talked her into.

"I feel like I've done something wrong. Look at us. Nobody wants to come here anymore. They think I'll infect them. Even our relatives don't visit as often. It's a miracle that Mama Benta stopped by today. She told me she's been giving the boys work . . . You must take care of your sister and brothers when I'm gone."

"Mama, don't worry about us. We'll be fine." I opened the ointment cap and started dressing the wound on her side.

"Make sure you go to your uncle or Mama Benta, whenever you need help. Don't forget your pride, but don't be stupid and starve either. And always be grateful for what others give you."

Her advice seemed like the opposite of what she had been teaching me for years—the opposite of our traditions. It was certainly the complete opposite of what I believed Dani would say. After all, Dani's motto was to take nothing from anyone. Not even an aroma.

"Auma," she continued, "listen carefully. I want you to work hard at school and make something of yourself. Don't get married before you're ready."

I nodded. It was a great comfort to know Mama had wanted for me the same thing I'd wanted for myself. Somehow, even after today, I would find a way to get that scholarship.

The lines around Mama's eyes relaxed. She looked at peace for the first time in months.

I got a clean, loose dress and helped her into it. Mama was so light and bony, it was like dressing a child. Then I tucked her back into bed. Under the blanket, she seemed to disappear. "I'll go and get you some food," I said. "I'll be back soon."

In less than an hour I returned with her meal and a lantern in hand. Without the sun's light, I struggled to make out her form. I couldn't see her chest moving up and down.

"Mama, are you awake?" I whispered. "It's time to eat."

No response. I walked over to the bedside and lifted the blanket off Mama's face.

"Mama, I have food for you. Wake up."

Only silence.

"Mama . . ." I bent closer to her, took her face with my hands, and turned it toward me. Her skin was cold. Her eyes were closed and lifeless.

I let go of her face and sat there for a moment, not daring to think the unthinkable.

I jumped to my feet and ran to the front door of the house, yelling, "Dani, Dani, come here! Mama isn't talking to me. She won't wake up!"

Dani came limping out of her hut and hurried into our house. Juma, Musa, and Baby had heard the commotion and ran inside behind Dani. They had all started wailing, not sure why I was crying. I stayed on the veranda while they rushed into the bedroom.

When my siblings came back out their cheeks were stained with straight, wet lines. I could hear Dani slapping the floor. She was wailing loudly, as if God himself had abandoned our home forever, just as she had done when her son, Baba, had died.

I wondered if she knew Baba's secret.

Baby sat on a chair, looking completely confused. She popped a thumb into her mouth, something she hadn't done in years. I gently pulled it out and wrapped my arms around her.

It was time for tradition now. It was my turn to scream into the night, asking, "What will I do without you?"

But Mama had told me exactly what I needed to do. She'd given me all the reason in the world to believe that I could do it.

The only thing I didn't know was *how* I was going to do it.

◆◆◆

After an hour or so, Dani finally stepped out into the doorway, looking confused. I looked up from where I sat on the veranda. I wondered why Dani had suddenly stopped wailing. Normally, Luo women wailed for hours, as we all had after Baba had died. At first the quiet was a small relief to me. But after a couple of minutes, the suspense began to haunt me. I sat there waiting for her to say something, but no words came.

Like a drunkard, Dani staggered toward the guava tree in front of the house. Then, without any warning, she loudly called out. "*WUOLOLO-LOLO, MAYO* . . ."

She gently but rapidly hit her mouth to produce the *WUOLOLO* sound. Then she bellowed the call for help repeatedly until she heard echoes come back from other village women. Within minutes, neighbors came running toward our home, some carrying flashlights, others lanterns.

Here they are, Mama, I thought. *The villagers are here. They haven't forgotten you.*

As more and more neighbors came, the brightness surrounding the house made it look like a false dawn. The lanterns lighting the compound reminded me of fireflies. Members of our church sang Christian songs, and the melodies helped steady me. For the first time in a while, I felt that God hadn't abandoned us. He was here right now.

For most of the night I ran errands, because people didn't know where things were. Most of these villagers hadn't been to our home in months, some even since Baba died half a year ago. There was a flurry of requests, and since Dani was mourning in isolation, I was the woman of the house. Someone asked if there were batteries for our small radio. Another wanted to know where the broom was. Several of them moved Mama's body out to the sitting room, then stripped the bed and took the sheets away for washing. The body would be taken to the mortuary tomorrow.

"You'd better hide anything that's easy to steal," said my cousin Tabitha briskly. "Your clothes, your schoolbooks. Come daylight this house will be full of guests. You'd be amazed at what people will help themselves to when no one's looking."

"I lost my favorite headscarf at a funeral," Mama Karen said, looking around for things to pick up and put away.

I wasn't too worried. We didn't own much worth stealing.

Mama Benta laid a hand on my shoulder. "Auma, we need you to keep this bedroom key. Be careful with it."

I looked up at the key, frowning. Of course our meager valuables in the bedroom—the radio and my parents' clothes—needed to be protected. But why had the women entrusted this key to me? Then I realized that I was the adult of the house now. Technically, Dani was the head of the family, but

Dani was too old to bear the full weight of that responsibility.

Gripping the key with both reluctance and acceptance, I went into the bedroom.

I had never fully noticed how small it was. The narrow bed took up half the room. In one corner stood an upright wooden box, and on top of that was an old suitcase that held Mama's clothes. At the end of the bed was the chair that Baba used to hang his coat on. And next to it, the stool where the lantern sat, lighting up the room. The single tiny window was slightly open; Mama liked to leave it open while she slept. Gently I pulled it closed.

Baby lay curled up on the floor, snoring. One of our relatives must have put her in here after dinner. I envied her ability to just dream the situation away. I crouched down and touched Baby's forehead, then got up and closed the door as quietly as I could. *Peace comes in sleep*, I thought.

At about four in the morning, the wailing subsided. People were getting tired. Some had dozed off while sitting up straight. Others had left to go back to their homes. I wasn't sure if I'd be able to fall asleep, but I decided to try. I went quietly to Mama's room and wrapped my arms around Baby.

When I opened my eyes and looked around, I thought: *Where am I? How did I get here?* I was confused and strangely frantic in the early morning light.

Then it all came shooting back: *Mama. Mama is gone. Mama died yesterday. We're in her room.*

I yawned and stretched. In the center of my palm, I saw an imprint where a small object had been pressed into the skin. I recognized the shape—a key.

I stared at my empty hand in shock. *Oh no!* The first responsibility I'd been given since Mama's death—my first job as head of the household—and I'd blown it.

I heard voices outside the house, soft wailing and commotions. I searched the blanket, trying not to wake Baby: no key. I scanned the floor: nothing. Tears poured down my face.

I wanted to go back to sleep and never wake up again.

"Auma, why are you crying? Why are people crying outside?" My sobbing had woken Baby.

I drew a deep breath. "Mama is gone," I said. "She won't be here for us again." Not everyone would have told a six-year-old the truth. But I loved my sister enough to answer her question honestly. I think my mother would have wanted me to.

"Are *you* going to be here with me, Auma?"

"I hope so," I said, giving the only honest answer I could.

"Okay. Take me outside. I'm scared."

"Baby." I wiped my tears and looked her straight in the eye. "I'm going to do my best to be like Mama. But sometimes, I'm going to make mistakes. If you promise to help me, things are going to be a lot better."

Baby looked even more confused. "Help you do what?" she asked.

"Well, right now, help me find the key so we can lock up the room when we leave."

Baby smiled. "You mean this key?" She held up a silver key that reflected the sunlight as she turned it back and forth. "I felt something poking me in the night, so I decided to hold on to it."

Trembling with relief, I took the key from Baby's thin fingers.

◆◆◆

The next day as I was running between the house and the kitchen to fetch something, I passed my brothers, who were piling wood next to the empty cowshed. Juma was saying to Musa, "I'm so glad we're getting so much help from the church even though we haven't gone in ages."

"Yes!" Musa smiled. "Pastor Joseph even talked to me and told me I was being a man."

Gratitude toward the pastor and the rest of the Christian congregation swelled inside me. I promised myself I would try to attend church more regularly after the burial.

"Let's take comfort from having such help now. Soon enough we'll be fending for ourselves," said Juma, and Musa nodded solemnly. My brothers were no longer little boys, I realized. I wasn't the only one who'd had to grow up fast.

◆◆◆

"Are you ready?" asked Tabitha as she peeked into Mama's room. I had been trying to get dressed for the burial but floundered, lost in a black hole of grief. The week since Mama's death had seemed like an eternity.

"Yes, almost ready," I answered, hastily buttoning my dress. Mama Benta had insisted on buying me a new dress for the funeral. It was strange to wear clothing that fit me comfortably.

"Let me fix your belt." Tabitha turned me around and tied the belt neatly. "There, now you look fine."

The whole day felt like a desolate dream.

The ceremony was much like Baba's, only there were a lot fewer people at this one. At first, I wondered if it was because she was a woman. But then I remembered hearing far-off wailing on three other nights that week. Three other people in Koromo had died within days of Mama. Many villagers couldn't spare time to mourn her because they had their own dead to attend to.

The pastor began the outdoor service, and we joined the other relatives under the makeshift shelter that had been built to keep out the merciless sun. We sat on the chairs reserved for us. People who couldn't fit under the shelter tried to find shade under the trees that bordered the compound.

Abeth sat quietly with me. Like so many times before, silence was all I needed from her for comfort. She had been crying, too. I imagined she had cried for my mother as much as she'd cried for her parents and little sister. I was her sister too.

When the pastor finished praying and it was time to walk to the grave site, I couldn't get my legs to stand. It was as though bricks were piled in my lap.

I felt impossibly tired. Aunt Mary had to help me up. She kept her arms around me as I dragged my feet. Tabitha held a paper over my head to cover it from the unforgiving sun. Abeth carried Baby, who quickly fell asleep over her shoulder.

At the grave site the pastor continued to speak, but my ears felt as if there were wads of cotton in them. I heard only "And dust shall return to dust . . ." Appropriately, somebody placed a handful of dirt in my palm. I threw it on the lowered wooden casket and felt my body sink down to the ground after it.

◆◆◆

I woke up staring at a circle of wide-eyed faces. Someone was fanning me and calling my name.

"Auma, are you okay?" Aunt Mary was asking. "You fainted at the graveside."

I realized I was in the sitting room. And I felt wet. I looked down to see if I had urinated on the funeral dress that Mama Benta had brought for me, but realized that people had poured water on me to revive me.

As she helped me up she was shoved to the side by Abeth, who was sobbing violently. I looked at her as if she was out of her mind.

"Why are you crying, Abeth?"

"I thought you were going to die!" She threw her arms around my neck.

I certainly wanted to die. Mama was gone and here I was, going to pieces when everyone needed me to be strong. I had missed the entire shaking of the hands. Dani, Juma, Musa, and Baby must have already shared their sorrow with the entire family.

Over Abeth's head, my eyes caught a glimpse of a familiar face. It was Abuya. It seemed that every time I fell in the dirt, Abuya was somewhere nearby.

"Mos." He extended his hand to shake mine.

"Thank you," I whispered, embarrassed but grateful.

Juma later told me that the line had been long, that for a good half hour his hand got a pumping. He said that almost the entire school had come for that part, even the teachers. But by the time I revived, nearly everyone had left. There were just a few mourners in the makeshift shade. I wondered why Abuya stayed so long.

But I was supposed to be in charge, and I'd failed yet again. Was I ever going to get any of my responsibilities right?

CHAPTER 23

I slipped out of Mama's bed, which I now shared with Baby, and started getting ready for school. It had been weeks since Mama died, and it was already September, the beginning of the third term. The national exam was approaching fast.

I was glad to put on my too-tight uniform again. I was more determined than ever to do well on the national exams in November and get into secondary school. I'd promised Mama I would do it. At this point Mama's encouragement was propelling me forward to get through the year.

Everything about our lives had shifted since Mama passed. Baby and I slept in our parents' bedroom, and the boys slept on the mat on the living room floor. I figured there was no longer any need to keep the boys sleeping in the kitchen, away from the main house.

Dani had started spending more time with us. Since Mama and Baba were both gone, she seemed to feel obligated to eat with us every night. Sometimes, I wished she still ate in her hut. I knew she meant well, but none of us felt entirely comfortable around her.

So far we had enough food. Our relatives had left some money from funds raised during the funeral. Musa, Juma, and I were keeping the garden weeded so that the maize we had planted would grow well. But still, I'd been losing sleep, worrying about everyone's health and grades and school fees.

I wondered if this was how it felt to be a mother. I wondered if Mama had lain in bed every night, worrying like this.

The loneliness I felt without Mama and Baba, particularly Mama, also kept me awake. What a terrible friend loneliness was. It just wouldn't let me be.

But at least I could look forward to school. Abeth and my other friends would help me get through this. I had a few teachers who cared about me too. I ached for more school, to learn everything about the world and how it worked.

I won't let you down, Mama. And I won't let myself down.

◆◆◆

In the evening after school, I made sure dinner was ready early so that I could join my siblings on the veranda before dark. We sat together and talked about our days—school, our friends, what was going on with our relatives. Baby had her eyes on the gate, as if Mama and Baba would suddenly return home.

"Baby, what did Ms. Margret teach you today?" I asked. My voice sounded like Mama's in happier times.

"She taught counting. And she called me to come near her to read sentences. After I read she said, 'Good girl.' Am I good, Auma?" she asked.

"Yes, you are a very good girl."

"Will Mama be happy with me?"

"Y—yes, yes, Baby," I said, swallowing hard.

Musa stood up. "Mama is not coming back. Do you get it?" he burst out angrily. He picked up a stone and threw it toward the gate. I felt a fresh hole open up in my heart. There was nothing I could say to ease the pain of this moment. Mama must've felt like this too, when I kept looking to her for answers, expecting her to be able to make everything right somehow.

Juma put a hand on Musa's shoulder. "Let's go and bathe in the stream."

Musa clenched his jaw and nodded.

"Make sure you're back here in thirty minutes," I called out. I sounded exactly like Mama.

◆◆◆

In November I braced myself to take the national exams: two days of intense concentration. The rest of the students stayed home so that we had the school to ourselves. Our teachers were kept in the staff room and only showed up if requested by a proctor. We'd never met the proctors before, and they all seemed very stern and businesslike. They issued each of us a new sharp pencil and an eraser, warning us to be very cautious about bubbling in our answers. If our markings were sloppy, our answers might be misread and our scores could suffer. As they handed out the tests, I fiddled nervously with my pencil. My future depended on the outcome of this exam. The whole experience felt surreal, as if I were dreaming it.

I'd missed so much school that I had no idea if I'd even be able to answer all the questions. I would have to depend on what I'd learned before Mama's death. Taking a deep breath, I prayed for calm.

Time to start.

◆◆◆

Christmas came and went. I was officially done with Class Eight. I tried not to think about the fact that I might never set foot in a classroom again.

The boys took advantage of their holiday to pick up extra shifts working for the Bimas. But they still made time to help me around the house. They even went with me to the stream on laundry day. The boys would rinse after I washed the clothes, using rocks to scrub out the dirt and stains. I wanted to train them well, just in case they ever needed to do their own laundry. Life was too unpredictable.

Baby helped me fetch water from the stream, sweep the house and Dani's hut, and clean the kitchen. With food so scarce, we had nothing but porridge most days, so cooking was a fairly easy task. But sometimes Dani and I were able to pick wild vegetables that grew in the maize garden or forage for edible plants at the edge of our property, where the trees' shade kept the earth moist.

"Eee, Dani, I found some greens that look like *ododo*," I shouted one day as we combed the edges of the compound.

"Let me see." I held out some of the green

vegetables for her to examine. She plucked a leaf and brought it to her mouth, bit off a small piece, and chewed slowly. She tilted her head as if to listen to the taste. Then she smacked her tongue. "Yes, it is! Where did you find it?"

"Here," I said, pointing to a lush green patch under a tree.

Dani looked skyward. "Oh God, thank you, thank you for providing! We have food for today!"

Whenever good things happened, Dani always thanked God. I was glad that she talked to Him on our behalf. I certainly hadn't kept up with my promise. The days had become so routine and filled with chores, there were times I forgot about God completely.

"This will be our miracle patch," I said, and Dani gave me a rare smile. I knew we would only be able to harvest this secret garden for a month or two, until the dry season came and the leaves withered and died. But we would find some happiness in the small green leaves until then.

As we headed toward the kitchen, though, Dani sank into a quieter, more melancholy mood. She looked down thoughtfully, lifting one leg slowly and then the next, choosing where to step. I'd gotten used to seeing her this way. I often heard her lamenting about what this world had come to—where young people died and only children and old people were left. "Why didn't I die and your parents live?" she would ask, staring at the clouds.

Today she asked a different kind of question. She wasn't looking at the sky for an answer. She was speaking directly to me.

"Auma, after your test results are back, what will you do? You'll be fifteen this year. We don't have enough money for you to go to secondary school. We barely had enough to pay the younger children's school fees."

I had known this talk was coming. "Dani, I understand our situation."

"We'll have to find you something to do. Maybe I'll send you to your aunt's, so you can help her. I don't want you marrying one of these school dropouts around here."

I eyed her suspiciously. "Dani, are you saying I should go and work for someone for money, or are you saying you want me to get married?"

My grandmother kept her eyes on the ground. "Your job now is to do what will be helpful to all of us."

I tried to shape my response carefully and respect-fully. "Dani, I don't want to marry anyone, dropout or not . . ."

"Aumaaaa!" Someone was calling my name. It was coming from the road. I ran to the gate to see who was calling.

"Aumaaaa . . ."

It was Abeth. She was waving her hands up and down in excitement.

"What is it? Is something wrong?" I yelled to her.

"No, you made it, you made it! You passed! You got four hundred and ten points!"

Abeth was breathless. She must have run all the way here. "The test scores are posted at school! I went over there just to see them and your name's at the top of the list! You got the best score!"

I stood there, motionless. I hadn't even been sure I would pass, let alone get the highest grade.

"Are you okay? Say something!" Abeth prod-ded me.

What could I say? I wasn't sure how I was going to afford high school at this point.

I finally found my voice. "How did *you* do?"

She looked away and shrugged. "I didn't do as well, but I passed. I got three hundred and eighty points."

"That's good, Abeth, you did do well!" I said, putting my arm over her shoulder.

By now, my siblings had heard the commotion and rushed out of the house to meet us at the gate. "So you're going to secondary?" Musa asked, looking very serious for such a young boy. He eyed Dani, who continued shuffling up the road toward our gate as if nothing unusual was happening.

"I'm not sure yet," I said. "I have to wait and see if we can afford it."

Juma clapped me on the shoulder as if I were one of his school friends. "Our Auma's going to make something of herself someday, secondary school or not."

"Somebody come help me get this ododo ready for dinner!" Dani called briskly.

Musa shot me a smile. "We'll handle it, Auma." The boys had learned to cook surprisingly well.

My family disappeared into the kitchen while I stayed outside with Abeth.

"Auma," Abeth sighed. "Look, we both know we're not going to school ever again." Before I could respond, she added, "But it's nice to know we're smart enough to go, if we could. At least we have that in common to whine about together!"

I knew she was trying to cheer me up, but I felt

as if my soul was shriveling up. Abeth had always been the practical one—as much as she'd supported me, she'd also always been realistic about our future. And she was right, of course: high school was a long shot for both of us. "What are we going to do now?" I looked down at my thin, long fingers as if I could find an answer from them.

"Work for people who can pay us and then get married," Abeth said reasonably.

But I'd promised Mama I would do more with my life. I'd promised *myself.*

"You're giving up, right?" I couldn't keep the anger out of my voice. "Abeth, we will do something with our lives other than just get married. We're not even fifteen yet!"

"Auma, look here." Abeth grasped my shoulder and turned me toward her. "We thought we might go to secondary school when our parents were still alive. That was then. Now we're . . . well, kiye. Look at what's happened to this valley. Death is everywhere in Koromo. It's like the cloud of death is settled to stay. Last year alone in Class Eight, eighteen of us were orphans. Haven't you noticed that the kich jokes don't cross your ears much anymore? That's because almost everyone is a kich now, or fears becoming one soon. And the teachers don't tolerate the teasing anymore. Some of them have lost nephews, siblings, you know." I could tell that Abeth had thought about this a lot, while I'd been wrapped up in my own problems.

"There's no help for people like us. We have to go the way all other orphans have gone. Sussie, Atieno, Teresa, the list goes on. They're married already, and they look happy."

"Happy?" I said scornfully. "Did they tell you they were happy? Haven't you seen them at the market? They look pathetic, walking around with their swollen bellies. Sussie is pregnant already, and she's got four siblings to take care of. Does that sound like a happy life, Abeth?"

I was practically screaming by now. I didn't care if Dani could hear me in her hut. Or Juma or Musa from the kitchen. Or even Baby, who was in the house. Perfect—if Baby could hear me, all the better. This was a lesson she should learn young if she wanted to avoid the fate of other women in Koromo.

"I don't know that they're happy, maybe that word is too strong. But they have food every day, Auma. We're not sure we'll have food tomorrow!" Abeth lowered her voice. "My sister died, and I know

245

it's because she didn't have enough food. Her belly was so empty it swelled with air. When malaria hit she had no strength to fight it. Auma, I don't want to watch anyone starve to death again. Ever."

A pang of guilt hit my side. I imagined how horrible it must have been to watch her baby sister die of starvation.

"I know, Abeth. I—I'll think about it. We still have time. I'll find a solution other than getting married. Most of the men here are disappointing, anyway. They're either drunkards or something worse! Even if I wanted to marry, I wouldn't want to settle for just anyone."

She gave me a playful nudge. "Maybe you could sway Dani to look in Abuya's direction and arrange something."

"Oh, right," I scoffed. "In that case, who do *you* want to marry—Peter?"

At that we both started laughing. I was glad we had figured out how to laugh together, even though we disagreed.

That night I went to sleep determined to figure out my next move. Whatever I was going to do, I wanted to make Mama proud. I finally fell asleep. Without a plan. Planning a life was exhausting.

CHAPTER 24

One Wednesday morning in January, Dani got busy clearing the compound. She pulled weeds and moved dry twigs. She seemed to be putting things in order, but I didn't know for whom or what. I kept myself busy, having woken up before seven, made three trips to the stream, prepared porridge for my siblings for breakfast, and then sent them off to school.

I hadn't told Dani about the letter I'd gotten from the provincial high school.

It was an invitation letter, telling me about the school and offering me a spot there. A spot I couldn't afford. Without the money for tuition, it was just a meaningless piece of paper. I knew that was what Dani would think of it, anyway. But all day, my mind kept going back to it.

In the afternoon, Dani sent me to the market to buy soap, matches, and sugar with our meager savings from the boys' income. When I got back I saw Dani sitting in front of her hut with a guest. I went into the main house first, unloaded my bags, and came out to greet the visitor.

"Auma, this is Josef. He comes from down near the lake. Your aunt sent him to visit us."

Her voice sounded . . . traditional. Ancient. A knot formed in my stomach.

I politely extended my hand to him and said, "Thank you for visiting," and walked away.

As I took off, I heard Dani whisper that I was the eldest.

Only a week later, another visitor was "sent by my aunt." What an interest Aunt Mary seemed to have in our family all of a sudden! She had come to both funerals, but after Mama's burial, she hadn't visited us once. As far as I knew, even Tabitha, her own daughter, didn't hear from her much.

After the third man was "sent," I decided it was time to consult Abeth about these visits. When we were by ourselves at the stream, I asked her what she thought.

"I don't trust these men," I said. "When I greet

them, they have this . . . look on their faces. They gaze at me as if they already know me. I can tell Dani has been talking about me with them. Do you think it means . . . ?"

Abeth nodded solemnly. "The elders will do that when they want to choose a man for you." She glanced around to make sure we were still alone. "Think about it, Auma. She knows you hate anything to do with boys, men, marriage stuff. Everyone knows that by now. Your face wrinkles whenever the topic of marriage comes up. I bet she started the process without telling you because she didn't know how to talk to you about it."

I kicked the dirt hard. This was happening too soon. I hadn't even had a chance to come up with a plan to get my education.

I took the shortcut home and approached the compound at the back. As I went through a small gap in the trees near Dani's hut, I heard voices and stopped to listen.

"So you are the son of Isak?"

"Yes."

I hastily backtracked into the trees before they noticed my presence. This must be another man sent by Aunt Mary.

"You work in Kisumu? What do you do?" Dani asked.

"I'm a carpenter."

He works in a city. Who knew what kind of life he'd lived there? I couldn't believe Dani would consider letting him know me, letting him touch me. I couldn't trust anybody. Like Mr. Osogo had said, there was no way of knowing who was infected. Plenty of people didn't even know they had the disease. I wanted to stay alive and healthy as long as I could. Just the images of Mama and Baba going through their last days were enough to make me think of becoming a nun.

"Remember, my girl is still very young," Dani told him. "I want someone who can take care of her. I want her to have a place where she can have food to eat and help for her siblings. You know this new disease has affected the judgment of many young girls, and we have to guide them."

"Yes, ma'am, I can do that. I just want a good wife."

"Auma is hardworking. She is very well trained and also intelligent."

"Thank you, ma'am. I'll talk to my parents and her aunt, and I'll be back next week so we can talk some more. Meanwhile, please prepare the girl, so that she will accept my proposal."

I had heard quite enough. I turned around and tiptoed back around the compound to the main path. I wanted to be seen coming through the front gate.

I walked straight up to Dani and the man, my head held high. "How are you all doing?"

Dani smiled, clearly pleased that I was being civil to her guest. "Auma, this is Odoyo. He would like to talk to you. Please bring a chair and sit down."

I got a chair and sat next to Dani, dreading what they were going to say. My body tingled, a strangeness I'd never felt. Then it went numb, like all of my limbs had fallen asleep. I sat there listening in what felt like a stranger's body.

"Auma, my name is Odoyo. As your grandmother has told you, I'm interested in a relationship with you."

Dani had not told me anything. I swallowed hard and barely managed to nod.

"I'll be coming back in a week so I can get to know you better."

I wanted to scream. I felt completely alone.

After Odoyo left, Dani leveled her stern gaze at me. "Listen, my child, I think it's obvious that our family is in big trouble unless we find some help. You're old enough to take care of a man and be of help to your siblings."

At last I found my voice. "Dani, I'm not ready to get married. And marriage is not a solution to all our problems. Who says this man will actually take care of all of us?"

"Listen, I'm old and I have seen a lot. It will be okay."

"No, Dani, it will *not* be okay!" I burst out, anger overtaking my fear. "I've seen a lot too. I've seen girls get married and have to go and work in the fields, or take housekeeping jobs, just to survive . . ."

"A man who works in the city will be able to support you."

"But I want to support myself!"

"That's enough, Auma. I don't have time to listen to your self-centered fantasies. We have dinner to make and chores to do."

I could see that nothing I said would change Dani's mind. I would have to find another way to convince her to reconsider her plans.

That night after Dani retired to her hut, I gathered Juma, Musa, and Baby together on Mama and Baba's bed for an important meeting. I explained that Dani was trying to marry me off. "This is the plan. In one week's time, a man by the name Odoyo will come back here to finalize the marriage plans. I'm going to disappear for the day until he's gone. I don't want you to worry about me when no one can find me. Once he leaves, I'll come back."

"How will you know he's gone?" Baby asked, her eyes filling with tears.

I touched her head gently. "When he leaves, Musa or Juma can go tell Abeth. She'll know where to find me." I made them promise they wouldn't tell anyone about my plan. Even Baby agreed immediately.

She understood secrets now.

"Abeth, I need a place to hide out for a night," I told my friend the next day. "Can I use your parents' old house? And make sure your dani doesn't find out I'm sleeping there?"

She just stared at me without a word.

I rushed on. "I don't plan to stick around when

Odoyo comes to 'get to know me,' as he put it. I'll go back home after he leaves, but I want Dani to know that there is no way I am getting married now."

"Auma, why are you so stubborn about this?" Abeth pleaded. "The man works in Kisumu! He must make more than enough money for your family to eat well!"

"That's not the point! He could have the disease! And have you ever heard of a husband who lets his wife go to high school? I'm not ready to throw away my dreams yet." I felt anger rising within me. Everyone was right about the difficulty of staying in school. Yet I still couldn't fathom marriage as an alternative. I could not understand how any man who worked a menial job could feed both his and his wife's family. Odoyo did not have a well-paying job. Was marriage just the solution people came up with when they had no other ideas?

Abeth sighed. "Auma, you're determined, and I can't stop you. I'll do everything I can to help."

The evening before Odoyo was supposed to return, I told Dani I was just going to make one more trip to the stream. But instead, I headed to Abeth's compound, where I simply walked into her parents' house. Except for when Abeth's grandmother had guests, the building now sat unused. But it wasn't as run down as I had expected. The bed in the bedroom was covered with a bedsheet and a thin blanket. Narrow streams of light entered the house through the corners of the two windows—one in the sitting room and the other in the bedroom.

I sat on the bed and waited. After what seemed like hours, Abeth tapped on the bedroom window as we had agreed.

"Hey, here's something to eat," she said, pushing a banana into my hand. "Lock the door from the inside and try to ignore the bats. I'll be back tomorrow morning." And with that, she was gone. A few minutes later I heard her grandmother asking her to do some chores. Abeth's grandmother didn't sound like she had any suspicions about my being there.

When it got pitch dark, I crawled between the blanket and the sheet. I gazed into the darkness, wondering about the suffering that had taken place inside the house—particularly on the bed that I was now lying on. The thought that I was running away from death and crawling into this deathbed made me shiver. I told myself that this bed that had once carried death could not harm me. It was the living—those who carried death inside of them—who posed the real danger.

I closed my eyes, glad to be listening to the bats rather than discussing my future with somebody I didn't know. Surprisingly, the shrill sounds of the bats flying in and out lulled me to sleep, and the next thing I heard was a knocking at the door. I jumped out of bed wondering where I was.

"Auma, open up! It's already ten o'clock."

I rushed to unlock the door. Abeth walked in with a cup of porridge. "You look like a wreck."

"For a second I thought you were Odoyo. I was dreaming that he was chasing me, and I ran and locked myself in our house."

"Oh! My! My!" Abeth looked at me, her eyes full of pity. "You really are tormented by the thought of getting married to this Odoyo." She placed the cup of porridge in my hand. "Drink this. You must be hungry. It'll fill you up and calm your nerves."

I smiled at the thought of porridge solving my problems.

"Your dani sent Musa here to ask where you were. I told him I had no idea. My dani said the same thing—and your dani knows my dani wouldn't lie. So I think you're safe for now."

I spent the rest of the day in the hut, plotting my next move.

In the early evening, Abeth ducked her head back into the hut. "Musa was just here. He says Odoyo has come and gone. And your dani's furious with you."

I didn't know what Dani was going to do, but at least I was sure she was not going to kill me. And all I was trying to do was to stay alive.

◆◆◆

I let Musa get a head start on me before I left Abeth's compound. If we returned together, Dani would probably punish Musa as well as me.

So I approached our house alone, my heart thumping. Dani was standing next to her hut, seemingly far away in thought.

"Good evening, Dani," I said, my voice surprisingly calm. She just looked at me without responding, turned, and then went back into her hut.

I did my chores as if nothing had happened. At sunset my siblings came running through the gate, where they noticed the compound was swept clean, a sign that I was back. They dashed into the house and hugged me.

That night, after Dani was asleep, we had our meeting. They asked me where I was and what I did. I, in turn, asked them about Odoyo's visit.

"Auma," Baby said, pulling my dress, "thank you for coming back. I was a good girl while you were gone. Did you bring anything?"

"No, Baby, I didn't go far, but I'll buy you nguru when I go to the market," I assured her.

The next day I had to face Dani again, but I was not afraid. I had a plan to keep us alive.

◆◆◆

Dani came to the kitchen where I was cleaning the mess that had accumulated while I was gone. I was glad Musa and Juma could cook. They just didn't know how to keep the kitchen clean.

"So where have you been?" Dani asked, standing in the doorway. Without waiting for an answer she added, "Do you know what went through my head when you didn't come home last night? How was I to know that you hadn't run into some old man on the prowl for virgins? As far as I knew, anything could've happened to you."

I swallowed, suddenly realizing how much she

must've feared for me. Dani and I completely disagreed about how I should live my life, but that didn't mean she didn't love me. If anything, she was being this insistent about marrying me off *because* she loved me. As she saw it, she was doing what was best for me. If I was going to demand that she treat me as an adult, I would have to consider her feelings just as I wanted her to respect mine.

"I'm sorry I worried you, Dani," I said. "But I felt I had no choice. I hid because I don't want to marry Odoyo. And you wouldn't listen when I tried to tell you how I felt, so I figured I would have to find another way to make you understand."

"I'm only trying to do what's in your best interest—"

"No, Dani. If it was in my best interest, you would have asked me to be part of the plan for my future. I told you I want to go to school, and you didn't listen to me."

"Auma, you may get a scholarship to school, but what will your siblings eat while you're gone?"

"Getting married won't guarantee their security either. I might be dead in a year's time for all I know." I could not believe I was talking like this. "At least let me try and fail at school before going into marriage. Let me decide my future."

"I am the adult here and it is my job to help you make it."

"I'm sorry, Dani, but I'm doing what Mama and Baba would have wanted me to do—trying the school option first. If you let me work during holidays, I could make money and take care of the family and still go to school on scholarship."

Dani sniffed. "We'll have to see about that. If your ideas don't work, I'll have to take charge."

◆◆◆

I hurried to finish my chores so that I could put my plan into action. First, I went to the Bimas' and asked Mama Benta if she had any ideas of where I could find work. She suggested a few people: one who needed help at the market stand, and two families that worked at the local government office and were looking for house help. I went to visit the closer of the two families, about a mile away from our home. I told them my story—that I wanted to save money for my family to use while I was gone to school—and they agreed to pay me well for a full day's work.

Next I stopped by Mr. Ouma's house.

He stepped outside to talk to me, his arms crossed. "What brings Auma Onyango to my humble home?"

"Sir, I'm wondering if you can help me get a track scholarship to go to secondary school next year. I got an invitation letter to Rawak Girls High School, and the province already has my name as a good runner, so if it isn't too much trouble—"

"I thought you decided you weren't continuing with school. I haven't heard from you since you took the exams."

"Sir, I didn't know what to do. I didn't know how to go about this. But I'm hoping you can help me get a scholarship before it's too late."

He gave me a thoughtful look. "It might be too late already. School will be starting in a few weeks. But I could use some help in my house from a charming girl like you."

Right away my antenna went up. Was he seriously offering me a job—or was this the kind of "house help" that ended in shame and even pregnancy? I remembered all the old rumors about him, which

I'd barely understood at the time. Disgust filled me. Even my own teacher didn't care that I was seeking an education. He was only interested in taking advantage of me.

I drew myself up. "Sir, I'm the best runner KaPeter has had in a long time. If I go to secondary school on a track scholarship, that will motivate other students to try out for KaPeter's track team. It will give people hope. The school is developing quite a reputation for having good runners, isn't it? I imagine you want to encourage students to join the team and do their very best. If I get into secondary school, I'll make sure to tell people how much being on our track team helped me."

His eyes flashed with interest. I knew how much he wanted his track team to be known as the best in the province.

I wasn't finished, though. "And I'll make sure to tell the girls," I added, "that the rumors about you aren't true. That you treat your students very well and that they have no reason to distrust you."

I had no intention of telling anyone that. But Mr. Ouma would understand what I really meant: that I could tell people the exact opposite. The community wouldn't look kindly on him for trying to seduce young girls. For years, my peers had gossiped about his behavior in whispers, never officially complaining to anyone in authority. But I could raise my voice above a whisper and expose him.

As my words sank in, I saw his face grow more thoughtful. "I appreciate that, Auma. I'll see what I can do for you."

"Thank you, sir. Now if you'll excuse me, my grandmother is waiting for me at the market, so I have to get going," I lied.

I turned around and hurried away.

♦♦♦

Things happened so fast. I started working right away, and soon I was bringing home enough money that we could start saving again. And one evening, Musa came to meet me on my way home from work.

"Auma, you have a letter! The KaPeter principal sent a Class Eight student to deliver it."

He stood there watching my face as I tore open the letter. "Is it from a high school?"

My hands shook so hard I was afraid I would tear the paper. "Yes," I gasped. "From the best provincial school! And they're offering me a track scholarship!"

I hugged him. "Thank you, Musa! Thank you for bringing it to me right away!"

♦♦♦

"Abeth! Abeth!" I screamed, running toward her house. By the time I got there, I was so breathless I could hardly speak.

"I'm going," was all I could say.

"Where?" she asked, taking the letter from my hand and trying to read it.

I lay on the grass facing the sky, still breathing hard.

"I am going to Rawak Girls High School," I whispered, half to myself.

Abeth beamed. "Congratulations, Auma! And guess what? I'm going to secondary school too! St. Peter's Mixed High School, right around the corner."

"Really? That's amazing! But how will you afford it?"

"Some of our relatives offered to help out. I never expected it—I'd given up hope. Not like you, Auma. But now we both have a future!"

Abeth pulled me up and started leaping around. We jumped up and down together until we both fell on the grass laughing.

♦♦♦

The next week was full of preparations. I didn't have much to take with me. With the track scholarship taking care of my tuition, I needed to use the money I'd saved from my job to buy my uniforms and personal items. But I still needed more for transportation, notebooks, and writing materials. Again, I had to think of a way out—Dani wasn't going to help. I think she was tired of my stubbornness. She hadn't said much since the Odoyo incident. I had grown accustomed to her assumption that I was going to fail, but I had decided something: it wasn't failure if I tried.

I took the bus to Aunt Mary's home, about an hour's ride from Koromo. Over dinner, I explained my situation. I hadn't expected a great reception from her, but what I got was even worse than my conversations with Dani.

"So you want my help, do you?" she said coldly. "I tried to help you by sending Odoyo to you. And what kind of thanks did I get?"

"Aunty, I appreciated that," I said carefully. "But right now I don't need a husband, I need to continue my education—"

"You think you know better than the adults who care about you?"

"No, Aunty," I assured her. "I just—"

She cut me off. "Your grandmother wouldn't have *forced* you to marry immediately, you know. You would have negotiated to delay the marriage. But you're too hardheaded to be reasonable."

I sat there stone-quiet, wondering why I had even come. I thought to myself, *Hardheadedness is probably what one needs to survive—in Koromo and beyond.*

"I think it's rude and ungrateful, what you did. And now you expect me to give you some of my own family's hard-earned money, so that you can go off to school and abandon your family."

"I'm not abandoning my family," I said, fighting to keep my voice from rising. "And actually, I'm respecting Mama's wishes. She told me to stay in school—"

"Oh really?" she said with some sarcasm in her voice. "Well, she isn't here to see how you will get what you need. It is left to the living to help you."

"Yes, Aunty," I said respectfully. "I'll be very grateful if you can do this for me, just once."

Aunt Mary shook her head and stood up from the table, signaling that dinner was over. I helped clean up in silence. I was doing what I had been taught to do—respecting my elders.

But while I cleared the table, I wondered why most of the elders in my life failed to think of constructive solutions to problems. Mama, Dani, Aunt Mary—they all seemed to jump to the easiest solution or give up. I wondered whether I would have been in this situation if adults approached their problems differently. What if they talked openly about AIDS, so that everyone knew how it spread and how to avoid contracting it or passing it on? What if they thought seriously about the consequences for orphans after their parents' burials? They could at least make more coordinated efforts to collect food and money for us, instead of leaving us hungry.

I would not be that kind of adult. I would look for real solutions, even if they didn't come easily.

In the morning, my aunt sent me off with enough money for what I needed. I thanked her and left. And I promised myself that I would never ask for her help again.

♦♦♦

The night before I left for school, my siblings and I gathered in Mama and Baba's room. "Write to me while I'm gone," I urged them. Dani didn't know how to write, so I couldn't expect any letters from her. "Keep me updated on everything that's happening."

"We will if we can afford stamps," said Juma. My heart sank a little. Stamps would be an extravagance, with money so tight.

"Don't worry about us, Auma," Musa added, and I swelled with pride for him and Juma. I knew they would work hard and take care of our family. If I didn't hear from them at school, I'd just have to trust that everything was fine.

Baby started bouncing on the bed, and before long, we all joined her. Jumping on the bed was absolutely forbidden when our parents were alive. In fact, we had never even been allowed in this room much, except when ordered to get something. Now, for no good reason, that room was all ours to bounce around in.

It was the first time since Mama had died that I felt like a kid again, not a grown woman—not someone who was leaving home for the first time, as unsure as ever about what the future might bring.

CHAPTER 25

Rawak was one of the top provincial schools, and the teachers kept us busy. My days started early. The track team woke up before five to run cross-country, then came back by six thirty to prepare for class. Even though I had to get used to the longer distances, I loved running again, and I quickly made friends on the team. A second-year girl, Margret, was especially kind to me, though she could never replace Abeth.

I studied hard and got good grades in all my subjects. I had three meals a day, unlike when I was at home. I wished my siblings were here with me. I wondered how well they were eating.

In the late afternoons when class was over, we students did housekeeping tasks around the classroom buildings and dorms and worked to keep the compound clean. One afternoon as I was collecting water from the common tap, an older student named Scholastica sidled up to me.

"Hey, girl! You're a mono, aren't you?" she said haughtily.

I nodded. All the first-year students were called monos. The rule for monos was that you did everything you were told to do by any older student. And I'd heard some of my friends complain that Scholastica was one of the worst bullies among the second-year students.

"Move that miserable-looking pail out of my sight," she snapped.

Before I could reach my pail, she kicked it, sending it flying up in the air. As I went over to pick it up, she called me back.

"Come here, girl. I need help taking my water to the shower room." I knew better than to say anything back. Instead I took her pail of water as soon as it filled.

"And make it fast," she said as she walked behind me.

In the shower room, I placed the pail where she pointed. "Good job!" she said with a smug smile. "You know your place. I'll be needing more of your help soon."

I clenched my fists in anger but managed not to say anything disrespectful to her. But the next morning at track practice I was still furious about how Scholastica had treated me.

When I told Margret about it, I expected her to be sympathetic. But she just shrugged. "That happens to monos all the time. My first year, I had a lot of trouble with one girl. She picked me out as her 'friend,' but that just meant I had to do all her chores—washing her clothes, getting water for the shower, buying snacks for her. Some of the girls are kind about it, but plenty just enjoy humiliating the younger students."

"That's so unfair!" I said indignantly.

"Sure, but it's normal behavior in boarding schools."

"Maybe it wouldn't be if someone had the guts to complain to the teachers."

"Auma, it's not worth it. Girls like Scholastica will just give you a harder time if you whine about it. Stick with us"—she gestured at some of the other second-years on our team—"and you'll be fine. Focus on your studies and on the track team."

As much as I loved learning and running, Margret's advice didn't comfort me. I hadn't come here

271

to be treated like a servant or a fool. I missed Juma, Musa, and Baby. I missed Abeth a lot. She would've been as outraged by Scholastica's behavior as I was. And she would've defended me against anyone who treated me badly.

"I can't wait for the year to end," I muttered.

Margret rolled her eyes at me. "Seriously, Auma? You just had one bad experience, and now you're ready for the year to end? It's still only the first term."

I fell silent, deep in thought. The reality of being in school began to sink in.

Scholastica never bothered me again, though. I think Margret and my other second-year friends had something to do with that.

♦♦♦

The first week of April, the term ended and school closed for holidays. Despite my frustrations, I considered my first term of high school a success.

But when I got home, I saw that things had not gone as well with Musa, Juma, and Baby. Dani had run out of money, and they were scrambling to survive. Baby looked pale and skinny.

"Auma, do you know we eat only one meal a day now?" Baby whispered in my ear that evening, probably not wanting Dani to hear.

I tried not to let my dismay show on my face. I wondered if hunger was the reason for Baby's skin lesions. From what I could see, as soon as one dried up another bloomed. We were going to have to do something.

First I tried to start a conversation with my grandmother about our financial situation. "Dani," I said politely, "do you need me to go to the market tomorrow?"

"My child, where is the money for market goods? I only buy maize for grinding at the *posho* meal when we need it." She continued to remove the weeds that had been picked with the vegetables from our kitchen garden.

"Don't worry," Musa jumped in. "We're ready to go back to work full-time now that school is out." Juma nodded in agreement.

"And I'll ask around to see what odd jobs I can do while I'm home," I said.

That month, the three of us worked hard and saved up enough money to last for a while. On top of that, Musa and Juma promised to tend the garden and grow more produce during the three months I would be gone.

Still, I went back to school worried for my family's future.

♦♦♦

The second term flew by for me. The new biology teacher brought my favorite subject to life. We were learning about living and non-living things and their categories. I couldn't wait to learn about the human body, the stuff I would need to know to become a doctor. Math was smooth sailing for me, and I even helped some friends with the homework, making me popular among the first-years. Before I knew it, it was time to go home for the August holiday.

At home, I could see how Musa and Juma's work in the garden and house were taking a toll on them. They were struggling in school.

The day after I arrived, I beckoned to Juma to come and sit with me on the veranda. "Tell me, who's your favorite teacher?"

"This year? I think it's Mr. Odongo, the math teacher," he said, smiling.

"So how are you doing in other subjects? Let me see your report card."

I looked at his report card. He had made mostly Cs and an A in mathematics.

I'd never had grades this low, even when I was struggling to finish my schoolwork. "What happened?"

"I don't know," was all he could say.

I inspected Musa's and Baby's report cards too and all three were in the C range or worse. My heart sank at the thought of my siblings failing in school. They needed an education as much as I did. But how could I blame them for falling behind when they had so many other responsibilities? The boys had to work, tend the cattle, and take care of the garden. Baby had to handle household chores that I hadn't started doing until I was several years older: cooking, gathering firewood, fetching water. I couldn't blame Dani either. She was old and doing her best to keep the family together.

I went back to school for the last term of the year with a heavy heart, but I kept my place on the track team and even played volleyball. Even though I didn't know what was going to happen the next year, I stayed focused until it was time to go back home for Christmas break.

The first thing I noticed was that Baby's health hadn't improved. She kept complaining about her tummy aching, and often had diarrhea. Her skin lesions were still showing up.

"We'd have more money to feed her if you were working," Dani pointed out. "Or if . . ." I gave her a look that made her trail off. I wasn't going to settle for her solution. But I wasn't going to let my baby sister starve to death either. I needed to come up with a better plan.

◆◆◆

"Hello, Tabitha."

"Auma! Welcome back. How are you?"

"I'm fine, but I'm worried about Baby." I figured that if anyone knew how to keep children from starving, it was my cousin, who had been raising her son all on her own since her husband died.

"Oh yes, I've been thinking that she doesn't look good lately. Have you tried giving her porridge with dry ground fish in it?"

"I thought that was only for infants and toddlers."

"No, any child who can take it will do well. Make sure you feed her soft vegetables too."

I looked at Tabitha with fresh eyes. She still hadn't remarried and was working very hard to keep herself and her child alive. Yet on the whole, she seemed to be doing fine. Somehow, seeing her determination gave me strength. At least someone in Koromo refused to take the traditional route and do what was expected.

And sure enough, as soon as I started Baby on her new diet, she was back to her strong, bouncy self. All her lesions disappeared.

Abeth and I still went to the stream together a couple of times a week, but our schedules were very different now. I was working a lot to keep the family fed. Still, we kept a strict firewood collecting routine on Sundays, where we were able to catch up like we used to.

Abeth told me how most of the students in her school were generally from our area. She was one of a few who had done well on the national exam. We both agreed that overall, we liked high school. We could be independent and away from the depressing news at home. We came back only to learn that more people had died. Neither of us minded missing the funerals.

"Let me tell you," Abeth said one day as we

were collecting firewood, "since my school is mixed, boys and girls, the teachers have to work hard to keep us apart. We have rules, like when you're talking to a boy, you must stand a certain distance apart. One girl got a beating for standing too close to a boy."

"I would do very well in a school with those rules," I said.

"Well, I'd never switch to a girls' school. It would be so boring," Abeth said. "Noooo!" I protested, laughing. "You should see the kinds of fights that happen. One girl beat up the other because she said that the other girl was too proud, and she wanted to teach her a lesson."

"Really? When the girls fight at my school, the boys are there to separate them right away. And boys fight in their dorm, and we only hear about it afterward. In fact, they have to schedule the fight after lights-out."

"See? My school's clearly much more exciting than yours."

"But the boys in my class are so funny. There's never a dull moment. It reminds me of KaPeter."

I thought about that for a moment. "You know, I don't miss a thing about KaPeter."

Rawak wasn't perfect, but it offered me what I'd always wanted. A chance to do what I loved most. I wouldn't trade the past year for anything.

Except . . .

Deep inside I couldn't shake the fact that my family was depending on me. Before the start of the next school year I would have to choose between continuing with school and quitting to take care of them.

CHAPTER 26

After several nights of crying myself to sleep after my siblings had gone to bed, I decided to go and talk to Mrs. Okumu, my former English teacher. I needed advice from an adult, and I figured that, being educated, she might have a different way of seeing things. I hoped she could help me make a decision.

"Oh, I'm so proud of you for staying in school this year," was the first thing she said when I explained I had been back home for the holidays.

By now I was incredibly nervous about asking her advice. It was so rare for children to share family problems with adults who weren't related to them. Dani would've been mortified—would've said I was compromising my pride.

I felt my throat begin to tighten. I drew a deep breath to calm myself down.

"I'm wondering what I should do to help my family," I began. Then I explained that my family couldn't survive without my help.

"I want my siblings to be able to complete their schooling. Juma will be in Class Eight this year, and Musa will be in Class Six. They can't keep up decent grades and have a shot at high school if they're working all the time. If I quit and go to work full-time, they can work less and study more. Part of me thinks I should make the sacrifice for their sake. But part of me feels like I earned this opportunity to go to high school, and I shouldn't have to give up on it now."

Mrs. Okumu looked at me thoughtfully. "I see it in your eyes, Auma—you so badly want to get an education. But it seems that life is taking a different path for you and your family right now. Think about it this way—there are things in life that can wait and others that cannot."

My chest felt lighter as I absorbed her words. I still had good grades, so in theory I could return to high school sometime in the future. Maybe going to work didn't have to mean giving up on school forever. Maybe both paths could be part of my life.

"I know you'll make the right decision, Auma," said Mrs. Okumu. "Both for now, and for the future."

♦♦♦

That night I reached a decision. I would quit school for now and go to work so that my brothers could complete their schooling.

Once I'd made up my mind, my anguish faded into the background. It was a relief to know what I needed to do next.

Now I could start planning. I needed to find a good full-time job. I knew that in Nairobi, house-keeping jobs paid much better than in the village . . .

Nairobi. The city that had killed Baba. I had no illusions that life would be any easier there. But I had also learned that evil was everywhere. If I stayed in Koromo I would eventually end up married off, and even if I didn't contract AIDS from my husband and die, marriage would be a kind of death. It would be the end of the person I was—and of the person I wanted to become.

If I was going to risk death, I might as well do it in a place where the unexpected could happen. Maybe at least some of the city's unknowns would turn out to be good.

I sensed that it was time to "run away from Koromo," like Mama once said.

One week before school started, as I sat with Dani under the jwelu tree, I said, "Dani, I've decided to find a better job to help us survive."

"What kind of job?"

"Housekeeping."

"You already had one, and it didn't help much."

"This time I'll do it full-time—in Nairobi, where the pay is better."

Dani shot me a surprised look. "Do you mean you're ready to quit school?"

"Yes," I said steadily. "For now. I'll send home all the money I make at the end of each month, so Musa and Juma can stay focused on their studies."

She sat in silence for a few moments. I knew this was what she'd wanted all along—apart from my working, she'd always thought I'd have better marriage prospects in the city. And yet she didn't seem happy. "What do you know about Nairobi, child? We don't have any family there."

"No, but Mama Benta's daughter lives there. Amina, remember? Baba used to tell us about her all the time. I'm sure she'd be happy to help me get settled. I can ask Mama Benta where she lives. Mama Benta has been so kind to us during all of this. We can count on her family to lend us a hand."

"Hmm," said Dani. "Well, Auma, if you work full-time in the city, we might not have to keep asking other people for so much help. Let me think about it."

I smiled to myself. Dani was on my side again.

♦♦♦

Two days later, Dani said that I should plan to leave in January. I was excited and sad at the same time. I was going to leave my siblings and Abeth. Worst of all, I didn't know when I would be able to pick up school again. But being an adult meant that I had to do what was necessary for those I loved.

Abeth needed to know. So Sunday came, and we collected wood as usual, then just before we started moving the bundles, I told Abeth my plans.

All Abeth said was "I'm glad you'll still be here for a couple more weeks."

I reached for her hand. "You could come with me," I said before I could stop myself. "You could get a job in Nairobi too . . ."

"Oh, Auma." She drew back with tears in her eyes. "My dani would kill me if I decided to quit school, after our relatives have lent us so much money for my tuition."

I nodded, a knot rising in my throat. I'd known this would be her answer, but I'd had to ask. "I would never seriously expect you to give up school now, Abeth. I admire you so much. After everything you've been through, you're going to make it. You're going to graduate from high school and make something of yourself."

"I admire *you*," Abeth replied. "Going to a huge city full of strangers—and cars and complicated streets—where you could walk for days without getting from one end to the other. And where you wouldn't know whom to trust. Where do you get such courage?"

"Abeth, to me, getting married would be like killing every dream inside of me. The city is no greater risk. If I go to the city and I die, at least I won't have killed my own dreams. I'll have died trying."

She nodded, and I could see in her eyes that she respected my decision.

That day we parted in sadness.

◆◆◆

In the middle of January, I got ready to leave. There wasn't much to pack. Baba's small traveling bag held my two favorite dresses and the only other two that weren't torn or too small. I shoved in the only two pairs of underwear I owned and pieces of blanket that I would use when I was "going to the moon." I smiled to myself. I was certainly going on a long trip, but not quite that far.

I took Mama's leso from her suitcase. I would use the cloth wrap to keep me warm. Finally I slipped a small piece of paper into the bag. On it, I had written Amina's name and address—she lived in a neighborhood named Kibera—along with the numbers of the buses I should take and the market where Amina sold vegetables. The stories I'd heard about Kibera frightened me some. A lot of poor people lived there, so there was a lot of crime. But the memory of Odoyo's wide grin, his eyes close to my face, made me click Baba's travel bag shut.

Next I ran to Abeth's house. I found her cooking dinner in the tiny kitchen. "Tomorrow morning?" was all she said.

"Don't look so sad! I'll come back midyear to see everyone," I said, starting to tear up.

"Just stay," she whispered.

"I can't," I whispered back. Forcing a smile, I added, "And by the way, you can have Odoyo."

She let out a broken laugh. "No, he's yours. Come back and marry him anytime."

I hoped with all my heart that we would see each other again.

I hugged her. "Good-bye, my friend."

This time I did not run back home. I walked the whole way, my feet dragging weights of sadness and fear. But I knew I had to keep going.

That night my siblings and I had our family meeting after Dani went to sleep. The meeting wasn't secretive anymore, but we just liked to gather in our parents' bedroom. It felt like a commitment ceremony. I wanted to assure my siblings that they would be fine while I was gone.

Baby was the first to talk. "Auma, what will you bring us?" she said.

I thought of Baba's gifts and was glad Baby still remembered those happier times. "I'll work very hard so that you can have sugar in your porridge, some cocoa to drink, and more cooking oil. What else do you wish you had?"

"A nice long pencil like Sara's," Baby said in a tiny voice.

"A toy car to race the other boys at school," Musa smiled.

"A soccer ball that I don't have to keep repairing," Juma said with widening eyes. Thinking of the great possibilities, he reached out and touched my arm. Immediately, goose bumps raised the tiny hairs on my dark skin. The three of them were depending on me to make their dreams a reality. I'd known this all along, of course, but now I knew for certain that I wouldn't let them down. As frightened as I might be, I was determined not to fail.

CHAPTER 27

The next day I got up before sunrise. I hadn't slept much for fear of oversleeping and missing the bus. As I finished dressing, Dani gently knocked on our door and let herself in.

"Are you ready?"

"Yes," I whispered, trying not to wake the others.

"Here." She pressed some money in my hand. "This should take you to Nairobi, with some extra in case you need anything before you find a job and start getting paid."

"Thank you, Dani."

I rolled up the bills and tucked them in my shoe. Mama had taught me that this was the safest place to keep money.

"Auma, I know this isn't what you wanted," said

Dani quietly. "But I'm proud of everything you've done and everything you will do. Everything."

I swallowed back the knot in my throat. Not trusting myself to speak, I only nodded.

Then I picked up Baba's bag, but Dani motioned me to put it back down so she could say a prayer for journey mercies. Her prayer was one I had never heard before. She committed my life to God, along with everything I was going to do.

I closed my eyes, saying my own prayer in my head. I told God what I had gone through, and what I wanted to do with my life, as if He didn't know. I felt sad and sorry for leaving three siblings behind, even if I knew that leaving was best for them. I promised I'd work so hard that my employers would marvel at me. I also reminded Him I still wanted to be a doctor, even if school wasn't in my immediate future. I prayed that He'd let me keep my health and my focus, and that He'd lead me to good running paths in Nairobi, so I wouldn't lose my speed.

At last I opened my eyes.

I was ready to leave.

I turned back into the bedroom and with my free hand adjusted Baby's blanket one last time. I hugged

Dani one last time, then tiptoed past the sitting room where my brothers were deep asleep, opened the door, and stepped out of the house.

♦♦♦

I walked briskly along the path to the shopping center, where I would catch the bus. It was semi-dark and cold. The wind gave me goose bumps. From time to time I looked around over my shoulder. At one point I took a detour to avoid the village dogs.

Soon I could see my destination, the bus stop near the empty market. In the distance I heard the low rumbling of the bus.

As I drew closer, my heart pounded faster. The morning had warmed, but my skin was still chilled. I wrapped Mama's leso around me and held my small bag against my chest. A ticket agent sat at the bus stop, collecting cash from waiting passengers.

I took my money out of my shoe, minus the extra shillings, and handed it to him. He gave me my ticket and change just as the bus rolled up.

Aboard the bus, I found a seat toward the back and sat next to a middle-aged woman.

"You going to Nairobi?" she asked me.

"Yes, ma'am."

"Is this your first time?"

"Yes."

She smiled warmly. "What an adventure for you."

A moment later the bus conductor stood over us, ready to collect our receipts. I gave him my hand-written paper ticket. He studied it for a moment, looked at me, and then tore a corner off. "Are you traveling by yourself?" He raised one eyebrow.

I didn't know why he was asking such a question. I'd taken the bus to other villages before, and no one had cared whether I was alone.

"She's in my care," the lady next to me replied.

The bus conductor seemed satisfied with that response. Soon he was back at the front of the bus, and the driver was starting the engine again.

Suddenly, I saw a stout man in a white coat running toward the bus, waving his hand, motioning the bus not to leave. When the man reached the bus, he handed his fare to the driver and jumped aboard. He was panting like a dog, his chest heaving and his tongue almost hanging out of his mouth in between swallows. I noticed a stethoscope around his neck. He set his bag down at my feet and took the only open spot, across from me.

"Doctor Ajwoga, why such a rush today?" asked the lady beside me.

He laughed. "Tell me, when is a doctor not in a rush? In our business, speed is the difference between life and death." He added, "And we could certainly use a few more doctors who are better runners."

My ears perked up. The doctor must have noticed, because he flashed a wide smile at me. I felt an answering smile blossom on my face.

As the driver pulled toward the main highway, I felt as though the chaos was beginning to fall into place. At that moment I felt seated in the exact place I was meant to be, even if it was still an uncertain and unfamiliar place.

I realized I wasn't running away from Koromo, but running toward great possibilities. And that was a good enough reason to leave. As the sun rose higher in the sky and the bus picked up speed, I felt a brighter future approaching.

AUTHOR'S NOTE

When the first cases of HIV/AIDS in Kenya occurred in the mid-1980s, information about the disease was minimal at best. Denial and myths took the place of facts. It was a very confusing time for many people.

Growing up in Kenya in the '80s and '90s, I saw friends and relatives directly impacted by the disease. There were so many deaths. I, like Auma, had many unanswered questions—partly because information simply wasn't available, and partly because my society did not encourage open conversation about the disease.

In the mid '90s, more information about HIV/AIDS became available to the general public through radio programs and literature. This gave me an opportunity to understand more about the disease.

In the early 2000s, I was living in the United

States and pursuing a doctoral degree. As part of my doctoral research, I studied HIV/AIDS education in Kenyan schools. I returned to Kenya to interview educators and children. During this time I was struck by the widespread misconceptions, fears, and confusion about the disease, especially among adults. I came into close contact with very ill people whose children acted as their caregivers. I interviewed children who were living by themselves after losing both parents. These children had carried the huge burden of taking care of their sick parents, their siblings, and themselves, with no access to services that would help them cope physically or emotionally.

I was amazed at how strong these children were. Of course they struggled under the weight of depression and desperation—not to mention the threat of starvation—but life had to go on. Day after day they woke up determined to live, eat, and get an education. I was in turn energized by watching and listening to them.

In 2007 I became part of a team that provides a meal a day to HIV/AIDS orphans and partial orphans. It has been my privilege to do what little I can to help children Auma's age and younger make it—even if for just one more day.

My experiences working with these children and young adults, combined with my own memories of growing up in a Luo village, drove me to write this book. The characters in *Auma's Long Run* are fictional. Any resemblance to actual persons is coincidental. (Though the famous runners Abeth and Auma mention—Kipchoge Keino and Tegla Loroupe—are real.) References to cultural practices reflect my own experiences with and understanding of the Luo culture but should not be taken as the only interpretation of that culture.

In some sense I wrote the story of all of us—my story, the story of the girls and women I grew up around. I wanted to explore some of the issues that thread through the lives of women: a woman's place in society, relationships, marriage, childbearing, motherhood, strength, confidence, and respect. Above all I wanted to honor the resilience of HIV/AIDS orphans, many of whom overcome their trauma to grow up to be successful adults but have no platform to tell their stories. These caregivers are not hailed heroes in this novel, but they are heroes in real life.

Kenya still has one of the largest HIV epidemics in the world, with thousands of new cases each year.

As of 2015, nearly 2 million people were infected, and more than 1 million children were AIDS orphans. (Up-to-date statistics and other information about HIV/AIDS in Kenya is available on the United Nations AIDS website, www.unaids.org.) The work to educate people about the disease, treat existing cases, and prevent new cases continues.

This novel is my tribute to the friends, relatives, and others who have experienced the effects of this scourge—and who, like Auma, refuse to let a difficult past or present shape their future.

For their support, thanks to my husband, Lameck, and my children, Akinyi and Teddy. For getting me here, thanks to my agent, Rubin Pfeffer. I'm also grateful to Miranda Paul for helping me navigate the complex world of writing and publishing, and to Georgianna G. and Joyce Norman for their help.

ABOUT THE AUTHOR

Eucabeth Odhiambo is a professor of teacher education at Shippensburg University in Pennsylvania. As a classroom teacher she has taught all grades between kindergarten and middle school. This is her first novel.